T0284534

Come to Me

Bogdan Rusev

COME TO ME

Translated from the Bulgarian by Ekaterina Petrova

DALKEY ARCHIVE PRESS

McLean, IL / Dublin

Originally published in Bulgarian by Obsidian Publishers as *Ела при мен* in 2007.

Copyright © by Bogdan Rusev.

Translation copyright © by Ekaterina Petrova, 2019.

First edition, 2019.

All rights reserved.

Library of Congress Cataloging Number:2019952039

 Co-funded by the Creative Europe Programme
of the European Union

Dalkey Archive Press
McLean, IL / Dublin

Printed on permanent/durable acid-free paper.
www.dalkeyarchive.com

KOMM ZU MIR

I wish I was a hunter in search of different food . . .
I wish I was the animal which fits into that mood.
I wish I was a person with unlimited breath . . .
I wish I was a heartbeat that never comes to rest.

We reach the Strandja Mountain in the late afternoon.

"It's so mystical here," says Charlie.

His tone doesn't allow for any disagreement.

"Do you feel how very mystical it is?" he says, in the exaggerated manner that's so typical of him.

I ease off the gas pedal, and Gollum—which is what I've come to call the car—starts crawling along the uneven countryside road. I roll the window all the way down. The air is filled with the summer smell of burnt earth and dusty conifers. It's been a few hours since we've seen another car.

"Let's have a smoke," Vera says.

"Again?" Charlie says. "Fine, if we have to."

Vera rolls a joint and licks it before lighting it. I cautiously take a drag. The marijuana's caramel aroma and the drier scent of the cigarette that Charlie lights up a moment after get mixed with the other burnt smells already floating in the air—of soil, vegetation, plastic, and the overheated rubber and metal from the car.

"So, let me tell you a story," Charlie says, speaking a little faster. "One time, Zdravko and the Little Sprite caught a train from the Sofia Central Station. They kept switching trains until they got to the southernmost point in the

3

country that you can get to by train, let's say somewhere in the Rhodope Mountains."

"Who's the Little Sprite?" Vera asks.

"The Little Sprite is a girl," Charlie explains impatiently. "And when they got as far south as they possibly could, they got off the train with their big ugly backpacks and continued walking south on foot, until they got to the border. They spent the night there, right next to some frontier post, where a bunch of wacky draftees were stationed for their mandatory military service. These guys' state of mind was made even more pathological by the fact that they hadn't seen another human being in months. In the morning, Zdravko and the Little Sprite woke up and everything was fine—they hadn't heard any mournful howls in the night, nothing had scratched at the nylon walls of the tent that they lit with a flashlight from the inside; I'm sorry, but they just got a good night's sleep, that's all there was to it, then they had some plain crackers and a bottle of cheap red wine for breakfast, drank a little water, and turned left."

"They turned left?" I repeat mechanically.

We've barely had anything to eat all day. The marijuana spins sparkly cobwebs in my brain and an invisible projector casts a light on the road's potholes and crumbling pavement, which turns driving into a fine art.

"Yes, they turned left," Charlie says. "Toward the sea, man. That was their plan all along. Since they didn't want to get lost in the mystical valleys, hills, ridges, and no-man's-lands of the mystical Strandja Mountain, they walked all the way to the southern border and when they got there, they turned left—from that point on, all they had to do in order to get to the sea was just keep walking along the border."

Vera is lying on her back in the backseat and looking up at the trees that stretch along the road. Smiling his maniacal smile, Charlie suddenly turns to her. His dark eyes have become even darker.

"How are you doing back there, girl with the big feet?"

Vera gives him a smile that's either dreamy or tired, or both, but doesn't say anything. Charlie reaches back and caresses her bare, suntanned feet.

"Girl with the big feet," he repeats with the same tone he'd use if he were talking to a baby; that is, if any parents would ever display the criminal negligence of letting him near their baby.

"Then what?" Vera says.

"What, what?" Charlie asks politely.

"Then what happened?" she says. "To the boy and the girl."

Charlie methodically puts his cigarette out in the ashtray. It's overflowing with cigarette butts and a dried, dark brown apple core that we can't figure out how to remove in order to clean out the ashtray.

"Nothing happened," he says. "What could possibly happen? They got to the sea."

"And now the girl lives in Germany, doesn't she?" I ask.

Charlie gives an affirmative grunt and leans his head back against the seat.

"Woah," he says. "It's really very mystical here."

I start driving a little faster.

"Did you know that the grave of Orpheus is somewhere around here?" Vera says from the backseat.

"So is the grave of Bastet, the Egyptian cat goddess," Charlie says.

"What would Bastet, the Egyptian cat goddess, be doing in the Strandja Mountain?" I ask.

"Man, I don't know what Bastet, the Egyptian cat goddess, would be doing in the Strandja Mountain," Charlie says.

I shrug my shoulders. The road starts going down a series of long and lazy turns. In the orange-hued distance in front of us, some houses become visible.

"So, what village are we actually going to—Bulgari or Kosti?"

"We're going to Kosti," Charlie says. "The village of Bulgari is also very mystical, but Kosti is literally overflowing with mysticism—when you take a dump and flush the toilet, mysticism comes gushing out of the tank. Kosti's mayor is a five-hundred-year-old vampire who rules the land with an iron fist. And every Sunday, while watching the *Every Sunday* TV show, he drinks the blood of young infants, sacrificial lambs, and sacrificial polecats."

"Young infants—really, man?" I say.

"Kosti's whole population," Charlie continues with the resolve of a steamroller, "is made up of vampires and zombies. I suggest we try and get there before sunset because Kosti turns into quite an unpleasant place after dark."

"We'll be there in ten minutes," I reply.

"Good," Charlie says. "Because it gets quite unpleasant after dark."

There's no music in the car, ever since the cassette player choked on the last tape we tried to play. We haven't listened to any music for three days now, except for the Turkish radio stations at the little village pubs where we usually stop and get a bite to eat. The only audible sound now is the gentle smacking of the tires as they roll down the road.

"Let's have a smoke," Vera says.

By the time we get to Kosti, the sun has already disappeared behind the rocky ridges that surround the village on all sides. The streets are long and straight, the houses look well maintained, some of their yards have old Russian and Czech cars parked in them, and there's nobody around. I slow down and come to a stop in front of an expensive wooden house—two decorative street signs have been nailed to both sides of one of its corners. One sign says Forty-Second Street and the other, Fifth Avenue.

"And here resides," Charlie begins, but then gives up and completes his sentence smoothly, without skipping a beat. "I don't even know who resides here, man."

Vera takes out her camera and takes a picture. It's an analog camera, and nobody knows if there's actually any film in it. If there isn't, there's no point in Vera taking pictures and we'd need to stop somewhere and get some film; but the only way to know for sure is to open the camera and take a look inside. On the other hand, if there is film in it, opening it would expose the film and we'd lose all the pictures Vera has taken so far.

In the center of Kosti, there is a round square. In the center of the round square, there is a big empty circle, meticulously outlined by a curb. The circle is filled with smooth soil, but no grass or flowers are growing in it.

"This is where the *nestinari* do their dance," Vera explains. "They put burning embers inside the circle and the *nestinari* dance on top of them in their bare feet."

"You're saying they have a special, um, a special piece of furniture specifically intended for fire dancing?"

Vera nods and takes a picture. The camera clicks convincingly.

We get out of the car and stretch. I leave Gollum's windows down so it can air out. It's still very hot, but the shadows of the surrounding ridges are already crawling along the square, the tallest ones creeping up the walls of the houses across from us. Charlie walks up to a utility pole and starts reading the death notices posted on it.

"Mitra Bankova. No power can bring you back to us," he reads expressionlessly. "Our tears will never dry. Your loving sons, sister, and grandchildren. The memorial will take place on June 22, 2000."

Vera snorts and goes over to the other side of the square on her own, to check out the village store, which is closed.

"Nikola Totev," Charlie continues.

"Um," I interrupt. "Are you planning to read all of them out loud?"

"I'm getting acquainted, man," he explains, narrows his eyes against the smoke of his cigarette, and continues reading.

"We might be meeting some of these folks after dark," he adds over his shoulder.

Night falls on Kosti as imperceptibly as a cat someone's dropped down on our heads. By now, we're sitting down in the village square, drinking beer we've bought at the store, which has opened up in the meantime, smoking cigarettes, and watching as the place starts swarming with people. Time seems to skip, so none of us realizes the precise moment in which the deserted village has transformed into the lively center of some kind of festival, but there it is anyway: middle-aged people are all over the place, dressed in their Sunday-best sweat suits and greeting each other; grandmas are sitting on the benches, skeptically smiling their toothless smiles; men are glumly and rapidly getting drunk at the rectangular wooden table and faded plastic chairs in front of the store, casting sidelong glances at Vera in her Indian cotton skirt, beaded sandals, wooden bracelets, and silver toe rings; children are running around and shouting in a dialect we can't understand.

Vera goes to get some more beer while we take a bottle of *rakia* out of Gollum's trunk. In the schoolyard, which is covered in knee-high grass, a rope is used to make a circle and the people from the village gather around it, the shrieking sound of a *zurna* is heard, somebody starts beating a *tupan* drum in an inviting rhythm, some young guys go inside the circle and wrestle, the winner gets a live pig as a prize. Then we all go back to the square, where an enormous stack of wood now stands piled in the middle of the big circle, arranged in some incomprehensibly complicated manner, like a wooden idol or a Trojan Horse reenactment.

Kosti's mayor (who really is impossibly huge and fat, with a red ball instead of a head, a bigger ball instead of a body, two small, glazed, lifeless, shiny little balls instead of eyes, and a round, moist mouth) puts a torch to the wood and a fire flares up in the village square. The flames rush upward into the black sky and obscure the bright starts hanging above our heads, the drinking continues in full force, but the mountain's cool evening air seems to suck the alcohol out of our veins and carry it over into the woods, in order to share it with the nymphs and the other things around the village, so nobody actually gets so drunk as not to be able to have another beer while we wait for the fire to go out and for the wood to turn into embers that a few silent gypsies then smooth over with blackened iron harrows until the embers become a pulsating dark red fiery carpet.

"I walked over embers myself once," I say as we watch a skinny old man in a white shirt holding an icon of the Virgin Mary high above his head while dancing on top of the live coals and stirring them with his bare feet, which sends smoke up in the air. "Though not as hot as these, obviously."

"And it didn't hurt at all, right?" Vera asks.

"It hurt like hell," I say. "I couldn't walk for a whole week afterward."

I nod toward the old *nestinar* who's still walking over the embers and chanting prayers while moving the icon up and down in what appear to be constant bows to the sky and the fiery earth.

"So, this *nestinarstvo* business either runs in their families and they spend their whole life practicing it with, you know, a pure and faithful heart, or they only do it once a year and then spend the rest of it in bed, changing the bandages on their feet, and cursing the stupidity that made them take on the family business."

Vera is disappointed. As far as I can tell, she's mostly disappointed in Charlie and me. I finish my beer, put the bottle down on the ground by the curb where we're sitting, and start working up the strength to stand and go buy another one.

"Where are we going to sleep, actually?" Charlie suddenly asks.

We look at each other.

"Don't tell me we got drunk before finding a place to spend the night again?"

Gollum starts crawling along a potholed road that leads up and away from the village. For some reason we decide it would be better to sleep somewhere above, rather than below it. The racket from the *nestinari* festival dies down surprisingly fast once we start driving away from it, so the houses on the outskirts of the village are already enveloped in total silence and darkness. The light from the head-lights bounces off humps on the road, crumbling walls, and barbed wire fences, which momentarily appear out of the dark and then disappear again, as if we were taking pictures of them with a flash.

The road narrows and the tire tracks deepen. The shrubs by the road keep scratching the sides of the car. Trees hang low over us, so it's very dark too. At one point, the headlights catch the glowing yellow eyes of some kind of small-ish gray animal, which bears its teeth at us before running off into the shrubs.

"Isn't it kind of a dumb idea," Charlie wonders, "for us to spend the night out in the open and in total darkness right next to a vampire village?"

"When the vampires come, you can chase them away with your big wooden stake," I reply, then clench my jaw as the car suddenly slams into an especially deep hole, but then keeps going. "Maybe we should park here?"

"Let's go a little farther away from the village," Vera suggests, a little nervous.

"Is it because of the vampires, Vera-Vera?" Charlie says in that voice of his intended for babies, then turns around to caress her, but the car jolts again, and he hits his head against the roof.

"No, Charlie," Vera replies, a little irritated. "It's because everyone saw which way we were headed and I don't know what kinds of ideas the village guys might get in their heads once the music stops and they get even drunker than they already were."

I switch off the headlights and we continue driving in the darkness.

A few seconds later, we're able to see our surroundings again—the steep dirt road before us, the black trees and the silvery meadows on both sides. The moon is very big and white, and its light is drowning out the nearest stars.

I drive a little further along. The road gets even steeper.

"I'm stopping," I announce.

Charlie and Vera look around.

"I'm stopping," I repeat and turn the steering wheel to the left, so the car turns off the dirt road, plows into the grass, and comes to a halt on its own. I pull up the emergency brake and turn off the engine.

Everything grows quiet. The hot metal hood of the car starts making popping sounds as it cools down. The wind is sweeping over the mountain slopes and the trees are rustling. After some hesitation, the night birds slowly go back to making their strange noises.

"We can just sleep in the car," Charlie suggests. Vera snorts, opens the door, and slides out of the car. The slope we're on is so steep that the door slams shut on its own.

"That's bullshit," I reply. "We'll sleep outside, like the elves. It's going to be very cool, you'll see."

"I'm not going to sleep," Charlie announces. "I'm going to watch over you two. Like Aragorn, son of Arathorn. I'll sit by the dying fire, squint toward the eastern horizon, and smoke glumly with one hand while distractedly caressing my sword with the other."

"Oh, no," I object firmly. "If you're planning to jerk off, you should just stay in the car."

During the night, something comes up to us and sniffs around. I first sense some soft and cautious steps approaching, then hear the animal breathing through its mouth. I smell the faint scent of wet fur. Then one of us stirs, our sleeping bags' synthetic fabric rustles, and the thing runs off like a shadow.

"Give me a break," I say in the morning when I wake up and take in our surroundings.

On Vera's other side, Charlie also sits up, yawns, and rubs his eyes.

Gollum is parked at a ridiculous angle on the slope next to the potholed village road. The whole car is covered in a thick layer of condensation, which conceals the muddy wheel covers, the worn metal body, and the dirty windows beneath a matte gray shroud.

A small oak grove is located just a little ways away from us up on the slope. The oak trees stand tall and straight, spaced equidistantly from one another in an almost perfect circle. Most of them look like they're the same age. In the middle of the oak grove stands a square house with little windows and a flat roof.

"Twelve," Charlie says. "There's twelve oak trees."

We go to take a closer look at the grove. It's very quiet among the trees. Without thinking about it, I walk up to one of them and attempt to wrap my arms around it. Its bark is rough and hard, but I manage to find a comfortable position and press my ear against the trunk. It gets even quieter. Vera is also up and dizzily walking around among the trees.

"This is a chapel, man," says Charlie, who's approached the little house and now examines it. "This is the famous holy oak grove near Kosti, with its twelve holy oak trees. Pilgrims have been coming here from near and far to sleep under these trees since the Middle Ages."

"Why?"

"Because you get a great night's sleep when you sleep under the trees, man. And besides, when you wake up in the morning, you find you've been cured of all your ailments, and you've also dreamt that you have to, I don't know, go forth and defend the Holy Land from the infidels, for example."

"That sucks," I say. "If we'd known the grove was here, we could've slept under the trees too."

"Why, didn't you get a good night's sleep?"

"I did, but I didn't dream of anything."

"Maybe we can stay for another night," Vera suggests.

"Um, no," Charlie and I object simultaneously.

We have to give Gollum a little push in order to get it back onto the road. While Charlie and I are doing that, Vera starts rummaging through her magical fringed bag, which she never lets out of her sight. The bag always seems to contain such things as a lighter, a slightly crumpled cigarette, a flashlight, some gum, a pen, or an old key that doesn't open any particular door but serves as an excellent bottle opener whenever we can't find a corkscrew. This time Vera fishes out a small, half-empty bottle of water and a packet of wet wipes with exactly three wipes left in it. We wash up, climb into the car, drive back through the village—which now stands silent and deserted under the bright sunlight—and continue westward.

"So," Charlie says, "what's our plan? We're leaving Strandja and heading to the beach at Irakli, so you can drop us off and get to the Burgas airport in time to pick up Dena at eight tonight—is that correct?"

"Uh-huh."

"Just so you can spend a single day with her, before she goes back to Germany tomorrow?"

"Yes, Charlie. Thanks so very much for the reminder."

"No problem. Do you already know where you're going to go?"

"No."

"If I were you, I'd take her to . . ."

"Does it really matter where they go?" Vera interrupts from the backseat. "What matters is that they'll get to see each other. How long has it been since you last saw her?"

I don't need to calculate, because I already know the answer. Every day at 22:22, I know the exact number of days you and I haven't seen each other. Every time I see you after we've been apart for so long, I get surprised by the way you look—sometimes you seem shorter than I remember, or I'm suddenly reminded of how much I like your lips, or I notice for the first time (or so it seems to me) the steely gray hue in your green eyes or that single gray hair on your head.

"It's been over a year," I say to Vera now.

"And you almost missed each other this time around

too," Charlie says. "We could've still been stuck in that parking lot in Balchik, if the car key hadn't dried off in time."

A few days ago, a few hundred kilometers north of where we are now, we wound up at the Miss Balchik beauty pageant. At some point, the host asked everyone in the audience to jump into the pool with all the contestants. I, of course, jumped in and started dancing in the blue water with my arms around the cool and supple body of (as it turned out) the future Miss Balchik runner-up. Charlie and Vera clapped. A little while later, I realized that the pockets of my pants, now drenched in chlorine water, were filled not just with money, some papers, and my phone, but also contained the car key, which had that little button that went "peep" and opened the doors.

"Woah, man," Charlie says admiringly. "You end your year-long relationship with the wonderful Bozhana, just to spend one single day with your ex-girlfriend. Then you almost totally miss out on that day, too, just to spend one minute with Miss Balchik. It's great! Life throws such crazy shit at us! Such a dizzy dance of highs and lows that life pulls us into—that brilliant, indifferent magician!"

Sometimes I don't even know whom Charlie is trying to imitate.

The road starts to descend some hills, which are getting flatter and flatter. I can sense the sea is just around the corner of one of the upcoming turns—I'm certain of this with the same supernatural confidence of that little boy who wasn't born on the coast and once caught his first glimpse of the sea through a train window, and afterward only got to see it once a year, during his family's annual holiday.

"Time is just one way of measuring the situation," Charlie carries on after a while. "We should also take distance into account."

I know what he's about to say.

"Several hundred kilometers . . ."

"Several thousand kilometers," he interrupts me with an edifying tone. "If we also take the distance that Dena has had to travel in order to get here into account. Several thousand kilometers, whose final objective is to penetrate into another person by just a few centimeters."

"Nineteen centimeters," I specify.

Vera makes a sound from the back seat.

"Man, we're just like salmon," Charlie continues, without paying any attention to me. "Millions of years of evolution, and we still have to migrate across half the world and risk our lives in order to procreate."

"I don't think Dena and I will be doing any procreating this time around."

"There's the sea," Vera says.

An unmarked dirt road with deep tire tracks leads to the beach, and Gollum drives along with a certain aristocratic haughtiness and without getting stuck even once. The dirt road turns away from the panoramic highway, crosses a sun-drenched field, and finally sinks down among the trees of a small forest right by the beach. We pass a few people, some in couples and others on their own—they're wearing expensive but worn-out swimsuits and sandals, their hair is highlighted by the sun and matted in dreadlocks, their skin is the color of chocolate, and their green eyes are examining us with curious hostility. They're all moving in a way that seems to suggest they have a primordial right to be here, while we don't. I like that. It means the place we're going is a good one.

The road ends in an improvised parking lot, where about two dozen vehicles have been abandoned. Almost all of them share Gollum's age and appearance—small, stubborn, humble, loyal cars, originally designed for easy driving around Western Europe's capitals but now getting employed as jeeps on Bulgaria's back roads—their wheel covers and side mirrors might be missing, but they're generously embellished with stickers from skateboard, surf, and snowboard shops.

Vera slides out of the car lithely and opens the trunk to get her big, heavy backpack. Her usually languid body is now buzzing with energy, as if sensing it's about to find itself among others like it. We follow her down the path among the trees, which is enveloped in a curious mixture of forest and sea scents, with undertones of sunblock and a faraway suggestion of an open-air toilet.

"This would be a great location for a really cool movie," Charlie says as he follows her, smoking and looking around in all directions. "It starts like this: a nice young couple goes to the seaside. They're both interesting, fun, sexy, and not really sure if they still love each other, but they look so good together and they're so used to each other that unless something extreme happens, there's probably nothing that can tear them apart."

"Where exactly do they go?"

"To Nessebar," Charlie says, without skipping a beat. "So, all right, maybe choosing an exciting vacation spot isn't exactly their strong suit. But once they get there, they meet this really nice local guy, a little younger than them, who's like a fisherman or maybe a bartender at a beach bar, and he teaches them to surf and takes them around and shows them all these places. They become great friends and spend all their time together—the movie becomes kind of like that Spanish TV show we used to love when we were kids. Yeah, like *Blue Summer*, but for grownups. There's even going to be a night scene when the three of them go to some seedy bar, the locals start picking on the girl and pulling her this way and that, which is when our otherwise easygoing local guy loses his shit and beats the crap out of the other locals, you know, and then the three of them run off and go somewhere else to drink some more, and the guy's eyebrow is cut open and bleeding, but he says he's fine, and so on."

The trees get sparser and then come to an end at an ancient metal fence that must have been white once but is now stained by rust in every possible hue of orange and brown. We walk along it, looking for the gate.

"So, one day," Charlie continues, "the local guy borrows a yacht from someone he knows and the three of them go for a sail. So, they're out there, they're chatting, but then things suddenly get really tense. Don't forget the movie's very intimate, and there's just the three of them on this little white yacht, under the hot sun, and the only thing we can see all around them is the sea. And out on the yacht, it gradually becomes clear that the girl has been fucking the local guy for a while."

"When exactly?" Vera asks. "I thought the three of them spent all their time together?"

"We never find out," Charlie replies. "But our main dude, the girl's boyfriend, has actually known about it the whole time. So, he kills the other guy. And that's one crazy scene, with the camera shaking up and down and focusing on some totally pointless details, you can imagine it, right? And our guy, who up until that point hasn't been having that much fun, suddenly turns into some sort of demon and beats the crap out of the local guy, using—I don't know—the anchor, for example, or some hook that he stabs into his throat, or maybe into his ear."

"That's gross," Vera says.

"Yes," Charlie says excitedly. "And then he throws the other guy's body into the sea. Then suddenly, things take on a ridiculous turn, since neither of the other two knows how to steer the yacht. They have no idea where they are, the currents are dragging the yacht in all kinds of directions, and they only have half a bottle of mineral water and nowhere to hide from the sun. I guess they shouldn't have thrown the local guy overboard, since they could've eaten him, but oh well."

We get to a gate, Vera pushes it open, and the three of us step onto the beach. Charlie shuts up. We're standing on top of a tall dune and when we look to our right, we see the longest beach I've ever seen in my life stretching for kilometers. It reaches as far as the horizon, where we spot a rocky cape protruding into the sea, and we can't tell if there's another beach beyond it or not. Some woods cover the slopes behind the beach, and almost go as far as the sand. The waves are crashing on the shore, undisturbed. There isn't a single surfboard, a single Jet Ski, or a single paddleboat in the sea. Some individual tents and some tents grouped into small camps are scattered along the length of beach, all the way down to the faraway cape in the distance, but they are all separated by at least a hundred meters of empty space. At the foot of the dune, we see a roughly hammered-together wooden bar and hear calm, pulsating music, like the beating of a big heart, coming from it.

"Fucking hell," Vera says, like a little kid.

We go down to the bar to orient ourselves. Vera puts down her backpack, takes off her clothes, and runs toward the sea. The guy behind the bar, who's very tall and as dark as charcoal, with bright blue eyes and extremely white teeth, follows her with a gaze that contains that unattainable mixture of innocent amusement and casual desire reserved solely for those who spent three or four months at the beach every summer. Charlie and I sit at the bar. I order a crème de menthe with sparkling water and he orders a large vodka with lots of ice.

"Should I tell you what happens in the end?"

"Of course," I say.

"Four days later, a fishing schooner finally finds and rescues them," Charlie begins.

"Man, I never know what a 'fishing schooner' is, exactly."

"Me neither," he says. "But I'm pretty sure you'll know it when you see one. So, they find them under the glazed blue sky and then we cut directly to the ambulance taking them to the hospital, because they're super dehydrated and they've suffered third-degree burns. Or whatever degree is high enough for it to suck, I don't know how burn degrees work exactly. Oh, I forgot to mention that after our guy killed his girlfriend's lover, he and the girl didn't even exchange a single word. They just stopped speaking and then started getting burns and hallucinations and had nothing to say to each other anyway."

"Uh-huh," I concede. "That makes sense."

"So, when they're already in the ambulance," Charlie says and takes a thirsty sip of his vodka, "the girl feebly reaches out and holds the guy's hand. Her burnt fingers touch his fingers and all that. And that's how the movie ends."

We watch Vera bouncing up and down in the waves.

"I don't know," I say. "It sounds a little too Hollywood-y."

"All right, then," Charlie says. "I'll tell you a different story. This one's very much true, I saw a documentary about it on TV. A few years ago in the city of Varna, there lived a young man who was a bit superficial but otherwise quite likable and normal. To people like you and me, he might have seemed totally uncool, but he lived in peace and harmony with himself and his surroundings, frequented his neighborhood bar, went to the beach, and had some kind of a job in the city. All in all, he was a wonderful young man. Let's call him . . ."

Charlie trips up and takes a sip from his vodka.

"Svetlyo," I suggest.

"Excellent," Charlie approves. "So, one morning, Svetlyo, who liked to work out, decided to go for a run on the beach. He was jogging along when he spotted a paddleboat, which the lifeguards had forgotten to tie and lock up the night before. All the rest of the paddleboats were tied together, except for this one, which just stood there on the sand, and the waves gently bobbed it up and down. It was very early in the morning, around six a.m., so our friend Svetlyo thought, why not take the paddleboat into the sea for a while, and return it before the lifeguards even show up. He wasn't even that much into paddleboats actually, but he didn't want to miss the opportunity that life had presented him with, so to speak. And so, Svetlyo pushed the paddleboat into the sea and pedaled pretty far out into the water. When he eventually decided to turn around and head back to shore, he suddenly realized that the current was briskly carrying him in the direction of Odessa, and he could neither see the shore or knew which way to pedal. He tried to use the sun as a compass and so on, but have you ever tried getting oriented according to the sun when you're surrounded by a blue desert on all sides? And so, the more Svetlyo pedaled, the less he had any idea where we was. He should've probably stopped pedaling and saved his strength. And while our friends from the previous story at least had half a bottle of fresh water, Svetlyo didn't even have that. On top of everything, he was already dehydrated from jogging on the beach. But that's how it is when you get lost at sea in a paddleboat—it's hard to just sit there, do nothing, and try to not make things any worse; you can't help but insist on pedaling as hard as you can, just to keep on moving, even if you have no idea about the right direction."

Charlie falls silent and looks into his empty glass. We can no longer see Vera, who's probably swum far from the shore and is now floating on her back with her arms and legs outstretched, as she loves to do.

"And?" I ask.

"And nothing," he replies. "Four days later, a fishing schooner found him and rescued him, he was super-dehydrated and suffered I-don't-know-what-degree burns. They took him to the hospital straightaway, hooked him up to an IV, and he recovered. They even, as I already said, made a documentary about him. Though I'm not sure if being on TV helped him get laid more. I mean, I don't know if it's cool to get famous for stealing a paddleboat and getting dragged out to sea by the currents."

Vera comes back and the three of us pick up our backpacks and head down the beach toward the faraway cape in search of a place to pitch our tent. We walk by a few camps and see some naked, dark brown girls and boys with lazy smiles and quick eyes, stretched out and sunbathing on the sand. Vera wants us to go all the way to the end of the beach, but Charlie and I insist on staying closer to the bar and the car. It's so hot that by the time we're done pitching the tent and putting our stuff away in its questionable shade, my t-shirt is soaked in sweat. To our left, the horizon over the bar is overhung with some heavy black cumulus clouds, which are cinematically coming closer together.

"Let me tell you another true story," Charlie says, after we go for a swim in the sea. "A Bulgarian guy died last week while surfing off the coast of South Carolina."

A few seconds pass.

"He left behind a widow and a small child," Charlie carries on. "He was a thirty-six-year old IT specialist, went there as an immigrant."

"That sucks," Vera says. "I knew a guy who died while surfing too."

"Yeah, but not off the coast of South Carolina," Charlie points out. "Can't you see how that changes everything? Just a few years ago, the universal order of things would've made this kind of death impossible. The probability of a Bulgarian guy dying while surfing off the coast of South Carolina, in the United States of America, would've been equal to the probability of a deep-sea diver dying on the Moon, or of our very own Dimitar Blagoev, the founder of Socialism, to become . . ."

"UN Secretary-General," I finish his sentence.

"Yes," Charlie says, his eyes wide open. "Exactly. Every time something like that happens, the entire Universe shifts by a millimeter and a red light comes on somewhere. Every time a Bulgarian guy manages to drown while surfing off the coast of South Carolina, it makes Somebody up there look down on us and once again ask himself how we could possibly be such total idiots."

"Are you trying to say this was some kind of achievement?" I ask.

"That's exactly what I'm trying to say, man."

Charlie is on a roll. He's using his hands to dig around the sand, lifting fistfuls of it in the air, then letting it run between his fingers.

"This guy is the unsung hero, the prince of chaos. Maybe he went to South Carolina with his wife and child on purpose, just so he could fall off his surfboard and drown, as part of the grand plan of some secret revolutionary organization which has set out to change the Universe . . ."

I've been looking at the water for a while now, watching it change its color more quickly than I thought possible. Right in front of my eyes, the deep blue of the sea lightens to an almost grassy green. The enormous cumulus clouds descend over the shore and we can already see the silvery threads of rain connecting the clouds to the land below them. Lightning bolts are flashing inside the clouds, followed by the slower rumble of thunder.

The sun is still shining brightly over the beach, but the storm is moving right in our direction.

"We should probably put all our stuff inside the tent," I suggest hesitantly.

Nobody moves for a while. Then suddenly, all three of us jump up and start throwing our towels, t-shirts, and sneakers into the tent. The storm is so close now that we can see the blinding flashes of lightning, and hear the tearing of the sky and the deafening thunder that follows it almost all at once. Brought over by the wind, the first heavy, cold raindrops splash onto our skin, hit the nylon fabric of the tent, and stab the sand around us with such force that they send small clouds of dust flying into the air. When they hit the waves, the drops look like small pebbles pouring into the water.

Just before we go into the tent, Vera silently points toward the bar, which now stands two hundred meters closer to the storm's path than us.

The rain is beating down on it like shrapnel and the hurricane's first gust smashes into it with such force that it picks up and tosses an ice cream freezer onto the beach and starts rolling it toward the water. The dark-skinned bartender takes off running after it, but soon finds himself walking all over the shiny ice-cream wrappers scattered on the beach.

"I've always wanted to say this," Charlie declares, as we zip up the tent from the inside, just seconds before the storm reaches us, too. "Brace yourselves!"

The beach looks like the coast of Normandy after the Allied invasion. The tiny camps of the people who live here all summer—their fragile accumulations of small, improvised conveniences (fire pits, portable showers, awnings for the tents, vertical sticks of an unknown cult-like purpose with strings of seashells tied to them)—are scattered all over the beach and hopelessly jumbled together. The only thing remaining of the beach bar is the counter, while everything else belonging to it has been tossed as far as the water. One of the barstools has flown over a distance of about ten meters and landed in the sand at a particularly picturesque angle—it looks like a crashed spaceship illustration in a sci-fi book.

Gollum is almost completely buried in wet sand, tree leaves, broken branches, and all kinds of human-generated garbage—empty yogurt containers, crushed mineral water bottles, cigarette butts—but otherwise there's nothing wrong with it. I manage to get it back onto the road, then turn left and head south to Burgas. I open all the windows and, when I speed up, humidity and the sharp smell of crushed grass and ozone rush into the car.

The road descends in a series of smooth and wide turns, which Gollum flies along freewheelingly, without any need for me to press on the gas. I keep to the right lane, and I'm constantly being overtaken by silver and black Mercedeses, Audis, and BMWs, which flash their lights at me as they drive past at two hundred kilometers per hour.

Burgas is already visible in the distance ahead and, as always, its skyline reminds me of an American city from the movies—the high-rise apartment buildings resemble bluish skyscrapers leaping up and down along the length of the coast, while further out into the city's outskirts, the countless crooked fingers of the cranes in the port stretch toward the sky. The road passes through the salt works—those delicate systems made up of cement and shallow seawater, where some kind of a rough, everyday sacrament seems to be taking place. They look like rice fields so much that I almost expect to see Vietnamese peasants with conical hats and pants rolled up to their knees, but there's nobody there—apart from a flock of seagulls and some other smaller and darker birds that flutter from one cement path to the next.

I drive past a little gas station, which has three pumps and a green-and-yellow sign that says "Denitsa." Out of habit, I press on the brakes and Gollum obediently slows down, but then I let it fly forward again. My idea to take pictures of all the places that have the same name as you remained just that, an idea. Restaurants, kindergartens, neighborhood cafés—I wonder if the types of places that have your name can be used to draw any conclusions about you in particular.

I have the same name as a rarely frequented peak in the Sredna Gora Mountains and a very popular but terrible singer and TV-show host from the late '80s.

When I get out of the next turn, I can already see Burgas's Sarafovo Airport. The air-traffic control tower stands tall with the bold, clean lines of a structure built in the '70s—it has the same soaring angles as the logo of the Stewardess cigarette brand. But several modern charter planes are parked next to it now, which have brought hundreds, even thousands, of tourists to the all-inclusive Black Sea resorts. The gray bays along the coast have come alive again, even if just for the summer. The people we thought had left for good are now making use of their new fellow countrymen's cheap charter flights and organized tour groups to come back—even if it's just for a couple of weeks, just long enough to go to the dentist and see all their relatives. ("So, how's everything going over there? You already getting by in German?")

Back when I did my mandatory military service, all my vices left me one after the other on tiptoe, without saying goodbye. But now, as I wait in the airport's parking lot, leaning against Gollum's hood, I momentarily have to chase away the thought of going into the arrivals hall and buying some cigarettes. Instead of doing that, I get back in the car and exercise some kind of inhuman patience as I attempt to pull out the tape stuck in the broken cassette player. It takes some time, but I finally manage to get it out. It even turns out that the player is actually working. I wind the chewed-up part of the tape by hand and stick the cassette back in. The speakers in the front doors come back to life.

When I come out and lean against the car's hood again, I can hear the clear ring of the most majestic chords in all the music of the '90s: Underworld's "Born Slippy."

In the improbably blue sky, I see a white airplane descending toward the airport.

Everything changes.

Nothing ever really ends.

One day—if that notion is still applicable then, if at the end of time the cycle of light and darkness still exists, drawn by the stars and the planets that orbit around them—an inconceivably powerful force will roll up its sleeves, because the moment will have finally come. Maybe it won't be us, but some other beings, whom by then we'll have discovered across the vast empty spaces of the cosmos. Or maybe it'll still be us, though very different from now—all merged together into a single pulsating consciousness or evolved to the point of resembling present-day humans as much as we now resemble green euglena. Or maybe—and if we're being honest, this seems most likely to me—we'll be almost the same as we are now. Just like the humans who invented fire were almost the same as those who eventually walked on the Moon.

But one day, they—or we—will accomplish what we've been striving toward during all these tens and hundreds of millennia of our evolution.

Of course, death will have been long defeated by then. The absurd diseases with their clockwork mechanisms programmed into all life forms with the only aim of maintaining the balance in the planet's finite ecosystem will have become completely superfluous in the new, compliant, hospitable, and infinite universe of possibilities. Life is a crusade against non-living matter, and it will carry on for as long as needed, until even the last molecule at the end of the world bears a spark of consciousness.

But one day, we—they—will turn around, so as to reach out to all those who weren't fortunate enough to be born in the new era.

Each and every form of life leaves a clear imprint in the material world, through which it has passed before dying. This trace doesn't fade—it just gets mixed in with the traces of all the other lives, but its atoms and waves preserve its memory, like pieces of an enormous puzzle—mind-bogglingly numerous, but still finite. The mission to restore an individual life from all the traces that this particular life has left behind seems absurdly difficult and excruciating, but if you think about what we actually are and why we were put here, it's inevitable.

And one day, we'll wake up again.

And even if this day is millions or billions of years from now, and even if we wake up far away from the little star we know and remember from our former life, we won't know it, because time obeys us in our sleep.

And even if we wake up without the bodies we're used to, I'll find a way to embrace you.

ODE TO MY FAMILY

to my daughter

My FATHER SAYS he named me the way he did because back when I was born, that was the only way to get the communist authorities to spell the word *Bog*, or "God," with a capital letter.

My father, of course, says a lot of things. Like most men in my family, he lives to tell stories. According to family lore, he and my uncle spent their childhood causing constant mischief along the narrow streets of Veliko Tarnovo's Old Town, bathed in the long afternoons' mellow golden light, like in some socialist equivalent of an early Fellini film. But to me, these tales always seemed a little too well composed, filled with too many surprising twists, and a little too suspiciously devoid of an instructive ending in favor of an impressive punch line, for them to be true.

Take, for example, one of his favorites, which took place sometime in the '50s: my father and his little brother decided to steal some watermelons from the back of an open truck parked in front of the old post office. My dad, undoubtedly dressed in shorts and leather sandals and already wearing glasses, climbed into the back of the truck and tried to pick out a ripe watermelon by lifting the green cannonballs one by one, pressing his ear to their warm, smooth bark, and knocking on them with his finger. My uncle, dressed in my father's clothes from the previous year, stood behind the truck and waited for his brother to toss the ripest watermelon down. Of course, that was exactly when the truck driver appeared, climbed into the cabin without noticing them, and drove off at full speed. The truck headed down the street and toward the outskirts of the city, past the heap that was the Tsarevets Fortress (had it even been built by then?), maybe to the village of Arbanasi, beyond the dusty hills with their medieval names. Screaming in his little kid's voice, my uncle took off running after the truck, while my father—who was older and kept his cool—started throwing watermelons at him, but "the pathetic little kid" (it's my father telling the story, after all) failed to catch every single one, letting the ripe fruits fall and explode on the hot pavement.

Or another story from when they were a little older: one day, my dad and my uncle ran a wet comb through their hair, straightened the collars of their short-sleeved shirts, and started going from house to house down their street with all the touching earnestness they could muster. This happened sometime in the '60s, and the two boys went around asking their neighbors for spare change, which they claimed they were collecting for an initiative to change the name of their street from Dr. Long (an American pastor and one of the founders of the Methodist Church in Bulgaria) to the much trendier and far more inspiring Yuri Gagarin (who had recently become the first man to travel into outer space). The carefully planned scam, of course, was quickly discovered—after all, at that time their father, my grandfather, was working at the local paper and would've probably been among the first to know if such a name change was really happening. As a result, the boys were forced to give all the money back and apologize, then sent to bed with no supper. (My father, who always hated his mother's cooking, didn't mind at all.) Or—an alternative ending—the scam wasn't discovered, so the brothers went to the Turkish pastry shop next to the boys' high school and used the money to buy a whole tray of syrup-soaked *tulumba*, which they then shared with the rest of the other characters who regularly feature in their childhood tales: the lanky basketball player known as Popa, or "the Pope," who eventually became a surgeon, got married, and moved to the city of Plovdiv, and who now rolls his cigarettes with the help of a clever little contraption; the sneaky numismatist Forie, who after the fall of communism joined the Democratic Party and got himself a job as the head of the local archeology museum, under whose term the biggest coin robbery from the museum's treasury took place, which remains unsolved until today; and the slight and lazy Chocho, who got divorced five or six times and became such a pathological liar that when he says "Good day," you have to look up at the sky and make sure it's not actually nighttime.

Or the story about the theater and the curtain, which went like this: one day, all the students at my father's school got rounded up and taken to the theater en masse, to watch some glorious historical play about the fall of the Second

Bulgarian Empire or perhaps the Tarnovo Music Theater's legendary production of *The Gipsy Princess*—a kind of local version of *Les Misérables*, which had been put on every single week since the theater was founded and by this time was so well rehearsed that the actors and singers could perform their roles even while completely drunk, which they often did. So, my father and Popa—being the charming rascals that they were—decided to slip out and shoot some hoops while the rest of their clueless classmates sat there and died of boredom under the history teacher's vigilant gaze. In order to avoid getting caught, the two boys decided to slip out not through the theater's central foyer, but through some back door, which may even have had a sign that said "Unauthorized Entry Prohibited," then started feeling their way down a dark hallway. A minute later, naturally, the curtain went up and the lights came on, revealing the comically frozen figures of none other than my dad and the Pope in the middle of the stage, applause, thank you very much.

The next time my dad went up on stage sounds just as implausible. Already in high school, he became the youngest member of an amateur theater group that only accepted him because he was tall, lanky, and had striking sideburns and thick, dark curls, which made him especially well suited to play any romantic roles. (For his part, my father's sole reason for signing up was the fact that the theater group's members often got to miss school and travel around the country with a blue Chavdar bus owned by the theater.) In his first play, my father only had one line—wearing a butler's livery and carrying a silver tray, he had

to come onstage and, upon seeing the mistress of the house
sprawled on the ground, he had to drop the tray and . . .

BUTLER (frightened): Madam?

The same actually goes for Dad's later stories, from when
he was already studying Bulgarian Philology at the Veliko
Tarnovo University, but still rocking the sideburns men-
tioned earlier, though they were now supplemented by some
rebelliously long hair, a mustache, and bell-bottom jeans.
He regularly listened to "illegal" radio stations while skill-
fully managing to avoid falling into the claws of the moral
militsiya officials (whom I've always imagined looking like
the policemen from *The Troops of St. Tropez*), who lurked
around every corner, stamping the bare thighs of girls who
dared to wear miniskirts, slitting "unwholesome" jeans into
shreds with scissors, and cutting the hair of anyone who
wore it long, right then and there, with the aforementioned
scissors. Back then, my father was so skinny that even I
don't fit into the leather jackets he used to wear. Once, he
was eating a pastry and leaning against the wall at the university cafeteria, when Bogdan Bogdanov walked by—this
was probably 1970, and the man I'd eventually be named
after, though he wasn't aware of it at the time, was still a
young assistant professor of ancient Greek literature at the
Veliko Tarnovo University—and, feigning cool surprise,
he exclaimed:

"Borislav? You're actually consuming food?"

Mom used to tell a different story. According to her version, an old Renault ground to a halt in the center of the

Borovets mountain resort on a sunny day sometime in the late '70s. Its door opened. One long, elegant leg, topped by an absurdly short miniskirt appeared, slid out of the car, and was then followed by a second. The legs belonged to Mom, whose cousin had signed her up for a mountaineering summer camp as a way to get her out of the mandatory socialist youth labor brigades, disregarding the fact that Mom was afraid of heights and had never climbed a mountain in her life. Dad was there too, having signed up for the same mountaineering summer camp, for the same reason. He's there even now—leaning against the wall of the teahouse and staring at Mom underneath his long, wavy hair. He took one last drag from his cigarette, and then—using his right-hand thumb and index finger, both of which were impressively yellowed from the tobacco—tossed it with feigned indifference. That same evening, he asked ask her to have tea with cognac with him at the teahouse. That same evening—I remember finding that kind of resolve remarkable when I was young—he kissed her as he walked her back to her hotel.

Back then Mom used to be the big love and muse (I never figured out if that meant lover as well) of a certain Veliko Tarnovo painter—one of those artists with thick, paint-splattered beards who only live for their art and rarely utter a single word. He was significantly older than her and loved her madly. But when Mom came back from Borovets, she didn't love him anymore; she was already in love with my dad. Every day, upon leaving Grandma's house in the nearby town of Lyaskovets and just before getting on the bus to go to her university lectures in Veliko Tarnovo, she pulled her skirt, which normally went down to her knees, up to the middle of her thighs, and—with typical female dexterity—used her belt to keep it there, in effect turning it into an improvised miniskirt. Grandma would have surely gone mad if she ever saw her looking like that. Mom resembled Twiggy. The pictures from their wedding show that the bride didn't just get married in a miniskirted wedding dress, but also wore a blond wig.

When they graduated from college, Mom and Dad started working at a language center that taught Bulgarian to foreigners—people from Afghanistan and Vietnam who had to go through an intensive language course in order to then be able to study architecture and civil engineering in Bulgaria, before eventually going back to their own countries, where they were to participate in the construction of socialism. The language center was in Sliven, and I remember the blue rocks above the town, the enormous tree at the end of the pedestrian shopping street, where they used to take me for walks in my stroller, and the wind that never stopped.

My parents were getting such good salaries compared to what was average at the time that they managed to go on two honeymoons. The first one was to Paris. Once there, my dad insisted on going into a sex shop to check it out, while Mom—probably wearing her usual short skirt—stood outside and waited for him. A young, pleasant-looking Frenchman walked by, greeted her politely, then asked, "How much?" For their second honeymoon, they went to

Vienna—a favorite family joke used to be that I also went to Vienna with them, as Mom was already pregnant with me. When they were in Paris, they were invited over for dinner by my mom's cousin, who was living there. The guide of the tour group they were traveling with gave them permission to leave the group for a few hours, but held on to their passports as a precaution. The cousin—I've never even seen a picture of her, but always imagine her sporting bangs and a black beret and smoking a hand-rolled ciga-rette, like a beautiful fighter in la Résistance—asked them if they wanted to stay in France. Back then, emigrating from the Soviet Bloc was still a risky endeavor, but the cousin said they could apply for political asylum, which the French government would eventually, even if not enthusiastically, grant—they were, after all, a young, well-educated couple from Eastern Europe, and they had already crossed over to the other side of the Iron Curtain anyway.

Mom and Dad turned down the offer. I spent much my childhood being quietly angry at them for being too stupid and cowardly to do it. Later, I spent a big part of my adult life being grateful they didn't.

Either way, my earliest memories didn't end up being of the fog over the Seine and the gray heap that is Notre Dame emerging from it (or more likely, of the suburban concrete housing blocks, on which noisy Algerians spray paint their tribal memories of the savanna, giraffes, and lions).

Instead, my earliest memories are from Sliven: the cracked pavement of the abandoned airport's runway in the middle of the yellow cornfields, where red and white sports cars often raced; the enormous toy factory, where nice ladies in navy blue coats showed me big stuffed bunnies that banged on little drums (my father also worked as a photojournalist for the local paper); the smiling people with skin the color of ochre who lifted me in their arms, talked to me in their unfamiliar, cooing language, and put a cone-shaped straw hat on my head; and Grandma, Mom's mother, who brought me out to our apartment's balcony every time a gypsy wedding passed by on the street below, because I loved hearing the sounds of their *tupan* drums.

Once upon a time, Grandma Zlatka worked as a servant at the house of some count named Monteforte in Borovets, back when the resort was still known as Chamkoria and Tsar Boris III used to spend his summers in a modest country house there. Grandma was still a girl, probably around twelve, when one day she was asked to watch Count Monteforte's baby (we used to think she made the Count's name up until my father stumbled upon it in some old government documents while researching the history of the Balkan-Wars-era Postal Service) whom she then proceeded to accidentally drop on the ground. Fortunately, the baby didn't get hurt and since he was still too young to talk and there were no other witnesses, the incident should've gone unnoticed. But when his mother (the Countess Monteforte?) came home, the little shit greeted her with joyful shouts—"Bam, bam!"—and an outstretched arm that mimed the floor hitting his head repeatedly, thus insisting on sharing the fascinating occurrence. So, my

Grandma got a good licking, was let go, went back to her village, and, after some time, married my grandfather—my biological grandfather, whom I don't remember.

This was Grandpa Dimo, the son of Great-Grandfather Duko, who according to the family canon was a bourgeois entrepreneur from Sofia's Knyazhevo neighborhood. Back then, in the place of the no. 5 tram that goes through Knyazhevo today, there was a horse-drawn streetcar, which was the city's first means of public transportation. Rows of shops lined both sides of the streetcar's route, which I suppose were the equivalent of today's suburban shopping malls. Grandma claimed that Great-Grandfather Duko owned all the shops on one side of the tramline. Unfortunately, Great-Grandfather Duko, a humble and meticulous man, was not as skilled at matters of the heart as he was at matters of business, which is why he married Great-Grandmother Mitra.

For her part, Great-Grandmother Mitra was quite skilled at matters of the heart. She was very tall and terribly beautiful and used to dress according to the latest Parisian fashions. When she walked past her husband's row of shops, even the cobblestones melted with longing for her and the passersby greeted her by lifting their hats, under which their black thoughts slithered about. Great-Grandmother Mitra obviously did not find Great-Grandfather Duko to be a terribly exciting husband, which is why she began a love affair with a dashing German officer. A string of wild nights filled with glamorous dances and dark betrayal followed, until even Great-Grandfather Duko could no longer bear his clients' and partners' mocking looks and demanded that Great-Grandmother Mitra put an end to the humiliating liaison. A scandal of epic proportions unfolded, in accordance with the best nineteenth-century traditions: at some point in it, the two of them were screaming at each other so loudly that little Grandpa Dimo (who was eight at the time) ran out of the room and slammed the door with such force that it fell off its hinges.

Great-Grandmother Mitra left Great-Grandfather Duko and moved in with the dissolute Fritz. Disgusted with worldly existence, Great-Grandfather Duko left her half of his property (which, of course, she squandered away, then buried the officer, and eventually died alone and impoverished), quickly sold the other half off at no profit, and retreated to the Kremikovtsi Monastery, where he donated all his money to the monks, then completed his earthly path in a cassock and under a different name. (The stately granite tombstone that used to be at his grave sang his praises as a donor to the monastery, but when the communists nationalized the land, including the graveyard on the Kremikovtski hills, and tried to turn it into cropland, they plowed it all up with bulldozers and smashed not only the tombstones and the stone crosses to smithereens, but also the bones of the people who were buried there.)

So, perhaps it was under the influence of the traumatic events outlined above, or perhaps it wasn't, but Grandpa Dimo (Grandma Zlatka's first husband and the father of my mom and my favorite aunt) became a communist. He was one of those genuine communists, who believed in

the proletariat's ultimate victory, read Marx and Engels in
the original, regarded the methods of the Russians with a
certain degree of skepticism, and never became a peasant
or a partisan. Naturally, he was imprisoned and contracted
tuberculosis, as a matter of course. They invited him to join
the Bulgarian Communist Party's Central Committee and
asked him to head party and government organizations,
but he refused. He died at his desk, pen in hand, while
writing a sharply worded but constructively critical letter
to the local party committee.

Several years later, Grandma Zlatka married Grandpa
Marin—my second grandfather and my mom's stepdad,
who was a carpenter. According to the story, when Grandma
met him, he was still working for the railways and wore a
uniform with shiny gold buttons, which is what made her
notice him. Though I don't remember my biological grandfather, I remember Grandpa Marin. He was pretty great.

The first memory I have of my dad's parents is from
much later—sometime in the early to mid '80s, the legendary golden period of late socialism. We were at a birthday
party for Grandfather Alexander, who was turning sixty.
All his relatives, friends, and colleagues had gathered in
the video-cinema, which my dad had reluctantly opened
on a Sunday morning. I remember speeches being given,
cameras flashing, and a lot of words being exchanged that
I didn't understand. Grandfather Alexander was a writer
and journalist, the local paper's long-term editor in chief,
and the author of several short-story collections. I remember him as a slight and nimble man with careful, curious

eyes and a mustache, which he vainly dyed with black hair dye. Conversations at home only vaguely hinted at the fact that he took his role as a public figure way too seriously, and that the work meetings that usually ran late into the night were actually taking place in quite an intimate circle.

Grandmother Anastasia was too unflappable to be concerned with rumors. During her best years, she weighed twice as much as her husband and ruled over the kitchen and her offspring with one hand of iron and an ever-present bottle of sunflower oil in the other. Her most prized possession was the memory of the short-lived German presence in Veliko Tarnovo between the two world wars, and she always became visibly moved while recounting how clean and tidy the German soldiers had been. She hated the Russians and the USSR with the same kind of hygienic-aesthetic passion, claiming they were dirty drunks who never shaved. She found black people so repulsive she couldn't even watch them if they appeared on TV as, let's say, participants in some athletic competition ("Oh, just look at how his skin glistens!"). She was an old Tarnovo native, a supporter of Tsar Boris III, and an admirer of his son Simeon II, at least until he became Prime Minister. (At that point, she solemnly took the calendar with his portrait down from the wall and only grunted in disdain whenever his name came up.)

But out of all these legends, the brightest trace that still shines in my memory was cast by the projectors of the movie theater.

I remember the time Mom and Dad came to pick me up from kindergarten, where—while waiting in trepidation—I'd gotten the temporary status of a prince, or even a god, since I already knew (and had told the other kids) what movie my parents were going to take me to see. *Super Monster* was an absurd Japanese fantasy film about a giant turtle named Gamera that goes into battle with a whole series of ever more terrible monsters as enormous as her (and sometimes even bigger), in order to defend Tokyo and the little Japanese people running around it. Somewhere in our family albums, there's a picture of me, looking hopeful and staring into the camera while clutching cardboard cutouts of two of the monsters, which my dad had drawn and colored in himself—this was during the innocent era before the appearance of McDonald's and its happy meals containing action figures.

I remember once coming back to Veliko Tarnovo after a holiday at the seaside, passing by the movie theater, and seeing that the poster for *The Empire Strikes Back* was already up—it was painted by the artist whose job consisted of making the movie posters by hand, and it showed Yoda looking down wisely and a little worriedly at the title of the film, which the artist had spelled wrong. (That's approximately when my firm conviction that all artists are idiots, probably engrained in me by my father, came about.) I remember, years later, going to see *Return of the Jedi* every single day over an entire glorious week: all I had to do was show up at the movie theater and say "I'm the son of Borislav from the video-cinema," and those magic words were enough to get me in without a ticket, in exchange for the promise to say hello to my dad. It was as though I was the son of some ancient exiled king and the mere mention of his name was enough to reinstate me as my magic palace's ruler.

I remember *Indiana Jones and the Temple of Doom* and that moment when the evil high priests chants "calmia-shack-tea-day" (which everyone hears differently, of course) as he rips out his rock-chained victim's heart—or this is what I'm guessing he was doing, since I'd always shut my eyes during that scene, and what I pictured in the darkness behind my closed eyelids, while listening to the poor Hindu man screaming in pain and terror, was probably much more terrible than what was actually happening on the screen. I would then open my eyes and see the high priest holding the throbbing heart in the palm of his hand, which for some reason pulsated with an orange light.

I also remember this one movie about a bus that wasn't supposed to go slower than eighty kilometers per hour, or it would blow up together with all the passengers. I remember the poster that hung on the wall in my room—Keanu Reeves with that cautious Buddha gaze of his that seemed to say, "I know you're scared but everything's going to be all right—I'm a little scared, too, but I'll do everything in my power to save us"; that ridiculous bus flying out of the flames behind him; and that word, written in red all caps, slightly tipped to the right, presumably from the quick acceleration. One single word that over the next ten years was going to take on a whole new, mind-boggling meaning.

Speed.
Welcome to the '90s.

In the personal mythology of my peers, high school was the most brilliant period of their lives—the golden era, followed by the unexpectedly quick ascent into maturity, the deterioration during their university years, and the new dawn of getting married and having their first kid. Splendid parties, experimenting with drugs, threesomes, family fights, renting an apartment and living alone, garage punk band concerts; long hair, stretchy jeans, and sets of keys tied to a loop in their boots for the Guns N' Roses fans; dramatic bangs, desert boots, and a theatrical kind of melancholy for the goths ("Dr. Bob will Cure you."); ripped jeans, flannel shirts, and totally unwarranted anger against society for the brand new Nirvana fans ("Grunge means never having to brush your teeth," Kurt Cobain). I went to school with a girl who was infamous, to her barely concealed satisfaction, for giving the best under-the-table blowjobs at the trendiest rock club in Veliko Tarnovo's Old Town; another girl used to go out with a legendary lanky dude, known as Pero the Penis, and then got pregnant, but not with his baby; a guy from my class was expelled from school because he used to get high as a kite on trihexyphenidyl and once, in biology class (during a lecture on the human excretory system), felt the need to share how easy and even pleasant it was to stick a permanent marker up one's ass; while another guy I went to school with was in trouble with the police over stabbing a ticket seller at the train station.

High school was a magnificent soap opera that unfolded all around me, in which my classmates fell in and out of love, slept with one another, got drunk until they puked, then puked some more, and kept on drinking. As a background to all this, the Iron Curtain was crumbling apocalyptically, the democratic protests were bringing thousands of people out to the streets, while my father concisely explained that we weren't going to catch up to the West as quickly as we liked, and that we'd need at least five or six years to do it. To be honest, I didn't believe him at all: five or six years seemed like such a long time.

I'm probably forgetting a lot of things. Medical research may turn out to be right—the abuse of stimulants may actually lead to short-term memory loss. It's either that, or the subsequent years turned out to be so much more interesting that they overshadowed the glamor of that time. Back in those days, I hated my name and the way I looked with such passion—I was lanky and skinny, my ears were shaped like jug handles, and I wore ugly, high prescription glasses—that I'm nowhere be seen in any of my high school photos. (With the exception of an obviously staged picture from prom, which shows me playing pool with a stunning brunette: my jacket's off and I'm wearing suspenders and a white shirt with the sleeves rolled up; she's gracefully sitting on the edge of the pool table and, with her eyes half closed, watching me as I'm about to make my next virtuoso shot. As far as I can remember, she was actually somebody else's girlfriend and beat me at the game.)

But whenever I think back on high school, the same

scene always appears before me: I'm at a party, wearing my glasses and one of my infamous flannel shirts, standing in the corner, and holding a plastic cup of vodka mixed with Coke. Everything is fine, of course, but I actually wouldn't mind getting up and leaving right then and there. I'm observing. I'm waiting. My time will come too.

*

My exam to get into Sofia University was in English and I got an almost perfect score on it, which was reported on the evening news. I was starting to figure out that the secret wasn't actually about discovering your true calling and putting all of your efforts and talent into its pursuit; rather, it was about finding the weakest point in the system and putting a maximum amount of pressure on it.

The university was everything I could wish for—a neo-classical monster in the center of the city, which sprawled between the National Library, the artists' hangout spots, and the country's trendiest dance club. The university had enormous ceremonial halls, where historical events took place, student unrests arose, and *Dangerous Liaisons* was screened; it also had tiny, oddly shaped spaces, hidden deep inside the labyrinths on the top floor, which we used to call "the Rookery" and which we reached by a different route every time, as if the absurdly narrow hallways and the rooms without a single right angle in them were constantly moving around on their own accord. There were also the young and ambitious assistant professors with beautifully kempt beards, daring scarves, and even more daring plans to change the whole world, beginning with the depths of grammatical structures—they got a kick out of having us analyze the dirtiest graffiti they could find in Sofia's underground passes and public toilets. There were the ancient wise men, too, with their wool cardigans, their skin like parchment, and a cunning glint in their eyes, which they employed in order to see through the surface of our young lives, so as to silently determine who among us carried more of the Force—their more discreet entertainment consisted of quoting authors and critics in the original, regardless of what language the original was in. There were the reserved, inattentive, and distracted ladies who dressed like little girls and absentmindedly stared somewhere over our heads whenever the dull requirements of everyday life, such as exams, grades, attendance, or the names of their students needed to be discussed, but whose light-colored eyes suddenly came into laser-sharp focus the moment they got the opportunity to shed some light onto the darkest corners of Latin or Old English, which is what they lived for. There were also the ruddy, loud, chubby teachers with fireball energy, who were besotted with pale, long-dead poets from the late Romantic period—they would jump from bench to bench while reciting those poets' passionate verses over and over again, day after day: life is short, art is eternal, a thing of beauty is a joy forever. There was an amateur theater group, too, where amateur directors argued to death, got into physical fights, and then reconciled with amateur set designers, in order to finally put on a single performance with amateur actors. There were the philosophy department parties, where tall and dark students dressed in black, as if out of a Bergman film, used their pocketknives to open bottle after bottle of purple-colored wine while discussing ideal categories with pale and impressed philology majors who wore heavy eye makeup and smoked countless cheap cigarettes with inimitable skill and style.

But above all, there were the women.

The women were everywhere—in the university's lecture halls, up and down its corridors and in its courtyard, in the public transport and in the dorms. They were little girls, who wanted to try all the stuff they could only dream about in their hometowns. They were arrogant beauties, who had grown sick and tired of empty-headed thugs with wide shoulders and fast cars, and had nothing against being briefly charmed by someone with a deeper and more cunning mind. They were naive debutantes, who longed to believe every word they were told without thinking about the consequences while they surrendered themselves with a willingness that rivaled only their lack of experience. They were reserved, well-dressed girls with a discreet bourgeois charm, who were willing to grow up with you and make you love them your whole life.

As for myself, I was free to say I was whoever I wanted. What's more, I was free to become whatever I wanted—because it was the first time in my life that I was on my own, far away from my parents, free to choose my new friends, anonymous in the biggest city in my country. I could become something I designed and then carried out myself, one day at a time—I was free to decide what to read, what time to get up, whether to go to class at all. I could lie about my past, about my background, and even about my name. I was free to decide whether to keep my accent, to absorb like a sponge the syncretic language of the new first-generation Sofia citizens that gathered around me, or to emulate the way television hosts spoke in the National Television building, which was next door to the university. I was free to decide to dress in all black, or in all green, like the elves, or in all blue, like the bards. I was free to pick a sport from the stunningly diverse athletics department offerings—fencing? horse-back riding? yoga?—or I could decide to not do any sports at all and take up drinking or become a junkie instead. Everything was available, and in abundance. The possibilities were infinite.

We lived in Studentski Grad—a big neighborhood on Sofia's outskirts, whose entire population consisted of tens of thousands of people aged between eighteen and twenty-six. On the buses from there to the university in the center of the city, you were hard pressed to find an old person to give up your seat to, even if you wanted to. Everything in the neighborhood was open around the clock. People ate whenever and whatever they wanted, drank nonstop, and went to sleep at any point and place they decided they were tired and needed to get some rest. The only mild form of control that the state and the institutions ever exercised over us were the occasional surprise checks by the police— students who were caught sleeping in somebody else's dorm room had their student IDs confiscated and had to wait in a long line at the local police station, where all they had to do to get their IDs back was sign for them; there was no other penalty except for the lost time, of which we had more than enough anyway.

I drank a lot, but I was doing just fine. We usually got together and had vodka mixed with tap water and no ice— each of us would go through a bottle and a pack of cigarettes on his own, while we sat around, laughed at each other's jokes in raspy voices (there were new jokes every day), played cards, and listened to our old U2, Guns N' Roses, and Björk tapes from high school. Then we all eventually got up and headed back to our own rooms—I would often find myself crawling down the path that led to my dorm while puking in the grass next to it. Once, very politely, I passed and greeted a guy I knew from class who was crawling in the opposite direction and also puking.

In the morning, I would simply get up and go to class, my only punishment being a vague hint of a headache, which would be gone by lunchtime.

I was there when Stroezha opened up—I went there on the second night after its official opening and literally every single night for the next three or four years afterward, while the place was gradually turning into the city's most legendary drinking establishment and growing around us, as more and more new rooms and spaces were constantly added to it. What had began as a tentative joke when they first named the venue "the construction site"—because of its unfinished walls, a forgotten work boot on the ground, a bucket of dried cement in the corner—was quickly transforming into a style and a trademark of its own and even something resembling interior design, although nobody called it that at the time.

*

Stroezha was also where I saw something that was not from this world for the second time in my life.

One night I was drinking there with a girl called Ina. Her real name was probably Angelina, or Velina, or something like that, but this was right when one very trendy lifestyle journalist called Ina had appeared on the scene, so lots of girls started shortening their names to Ina. (The journalist's real name was actually Radostina.)

It was quite late, maybe three o'clock in the morning, and Stroezha's usual wild party was gradually unwinding to that particular point where all the seats at the many bars were still taken but people no longer had to climb on top of each other to get another dirt cheap drink. Ina and I were both drinking a cocktail called Japanese Morning, which consisted of vodka and red vermouth in equal measure with a slice of lemon, and which—throughout all the years I lived in Studentski Grad—was priced at something close to the equivalent of a dollar.

That's when two guys, a girl, and a dog walked in.

All four were very skinny. One of the guys was tall, while the other was short and somehow fragile. The girl was petite and had a large amount of black hair, in which snowflakes were glistening. They were all dressed more or less the same, with shapeless gray or black winter coats and skinny striped or checkered pants. Their boots were muddy from the snow outside. Despite its wet fur, the dog acted in a distinctly dignified manner and kept a slight distance from the group, as if it had found itself in it only recently and still hadn't decided whether it wanted to be perceived as a part of it or not.

The two guys and the girl calmly walked over to the middle of the venue and put their army-style canvas drawstring backpacks on the ground, then squatted next to them and started taking out silver balls, long knives, and some kind of sticks wrapped in black string. The dog took a walk around the room, found itself a spot underneath the chair of some guy whose mouth gaped open as he observed the whole scene, then lay down and rested its head on its front paws.

When the three of them stood up, all the lights in Stroezha went out.

The little tea light candles lining the bar tops suddenly started glowing more brightly in the velvety darkness.

The music stopped as well, and all conversations quieted down.

The girl picked up the silver balls from the ground and threw them in the air one by one. Before they could fall back down, she already had them spinning in a ghostly silvery circle. In the darkness, her hands remained invisible. Meanwhile, the two guys behind her started tossing the long knives back and forth to each other, their blades tracing fantastical figures in the candlelight.

The dog yawned.

Even the drunk students from the Technical University, who'd been the loudest until that moment, watched the jugglers with bated breath, as if under a spell. Ina found my hand underneath the bar and squeezed it. The sound of the balls and knives swishing through the air was heard distinctly in the otherwise quiet space.

This was happening at three o'clock in the morning, at a remote watering hole on the outskirts of the city, at the very beginning of the '90s. The phenomenon of street artists was still unheard of. None of us had ever seen jugglers anywhere else apart from the circus. Nobody from Stroezha's staff—and I know this because it was something that was talked about for years afterward—had arranged for the three strangers to come to the venue and perform.

Nobody ever saw them again.

After a while, the girl caught the balls one by one and put them back down on the floor by her feet. When she straightened back up, she was holding the torches. The guys lit them silently—the shorter one went over to the nearest bar and borrowed a light from a group of people who stood frozen like statues and could only follow him with their eyes.

The torches went flying into the air. This time, the noise that the flames made as they whizzed and twirled around in the hands of the girl was much more noticeable. While she juggled, the girl sent out heat waves around her with every twirl of the burning torches.

"I don't got it," Ina whispered, totally charmed.

I smiled in the darkness—so widely that my eyes narrowed to slits and the corners of my mouth stretched so far out, it was almost as though they were trying to touch my earlobes.

"Everything's all right," I said in a raspy voice. "It just means that everything is all right."

Because I'd only just come to realize—shortly before the guys and the girl quietly put their stuff away and walked out of Stroezha as calmly as they'd come in, without expecting any applause or making eye contact with anyone (the dog gave each of us a defiant look before turning around to follow them out)—what it was that I had just witnessed. The jugglers were a sign, a guiding light, and an assurance that Somebody was on our side too, and that he wasn't any less mighty than the Other One.

The Other One had made his presence clearly known several months earlier—that was the first time in my life that I saw something that was not from this world.

One evening, I took the bus from Sofia back home to Veliko Tarnovo. It was October—the weather was rainy and the days were getting shorter. This was going to be the first time I was seeing Mom and Dad since I'd gone off to university. There would be hugs, stories about what life was like in Sofia, and pleas "to pack some warm clothes, since there's no telling when you'll be back."

But before all that could take place, I got off the bus in the center of Veliko Turnovo and went to get the local bus that was going to take me home. At the bus stop, I sat on top of my bag and nodded at various acquaintances who walked by as I waited—it was Friday night and people were heading out to the bars in the Old Town.

That's when a guy from school came up to me—I recognized his face, though I didn't know his name. He'd been a year or two below me. He was obviously aware of what year I'd been in as well, because he asked me if I'd heard what happened to Stefan.

"No?"

Back in school, Stefan and I had shared a desk for five years.

"Well, he died," the guy said.

"Yeah, right."

"He was fixing some car," the guy explained. "He was lying under it, fixing something. The jackscrew gave in and broke. The car crushed him to death."

"Are you being serious?"

"Uh-huh."

"When?"

"I think it was yesterday. They haven't had the funeral yet."

"Well, okay," I said, because I didn't know what else to say. "Thanks for telling me."

"No problem," the guy said. "It sucks."

"It does suck," I repeated.

"He was always fixing cars, wasn't he . . ."

"He was."

"See you," the guy said and walked away.

I stood under the shelter of the bus stop and waited

a little longer. The rain had stopped. My bus was still nowhere to be seen.

I remembered how Stefan and I used to go clubbing together—I think the first time I'd gone clubbing in my life was actually with him. Sometimes we'd hide a bottle of wine in our jackets and try sneaking it into the club, because we didn't have enough money to get drinks from the bar. On the off chance we did have some money, it would only be enough for a small vodka in a plastic cup, which we would then proceed to ash in before drinking, since somebody had told us we'd get tipsier that way. Stefan was quite short, with extremely bowed but powerful legs, which didn't stop him from always wearing tight stretchy jeans and white sneakers, just like Axl Rose. Girls, for whatever reason, used to be into him—or in any case, they were into him more than they were into me. We were eighteen. It seemed to me absurd that he had died. Nobody had started dying yet. Even our grandparents were still alive.

Then I remembered something else as well. Stefan and I both had relatively strict parents, so we weren't allowed to stay out very late, especially not on school nights. When we did go out, we usually stayed at the bar until the last possible moment—fifteen minutes before our curfew, at which point we'd leave and run all the way home. This would let our clothes air out from the cigarette smoke and, besides, running "got all the cigarettes out of our lungs," as Stefan claimed. We must've had so much energy, to be able, after drinking all night, to run two or three kilometers for fifteen minutes without stopping.

I now stood up, picked up my bag, and put it over my shoulder. I decided that if I could just run all the way to Stefan's apartment building, it would all turn out to be some kind of horrible, stupid joke. He was probably not going to be in, since it was Friday night, and I'd simply walk home (without running) and forget about the whole thing.

I could do it. My bag wasn't heavy (it was filled mostly with clothes and bedsheets that needed to be washed), but it had an awkwardly long handle, so it kept sliding down my back and hitting my ass or the backsides of my knees. I kept tripping and couldn't keep an even pace or get my breathing under control, but still continued to run. Even though I was already out of breath after the first few hundred meters, I was determined I'd make it. Stefan didn't live that far away. The air was pleasantly cool after the rain and the streets in his neighborhood had very few people on them.

But then I spotted him—in the cone-shaped light cast by a streetlight right in front of his building, Stefan himself was walking toward me. There were still a hundred meters or so between the two of us, but I had no doubt it was him, with his bowed legs and that swagger that's typical of very short people who have very high self-confidence. I slowed down. He slowed down too, while he was still underneath the streetlight—perhaps he recognized me.

I stopped running. I walked toward him with my bag over my shoulder, just letting the relief wash over me, without asking myself any questions. ("What kind of idiot lies to somebody he barely knows that his high school best friend got crushed to death by a car? Why would you even do that? Something about the whole story was, off but what?!")

When we passed each other, the stranger gave me a fixed and lengthy look. From up close, he didn't look like Stefan at all. I don't think he even walked like him and his legs weren't even that bowed. He was almost as tall as me. I couldn't understand how I could mistake him for my best, and now dead, friend.

When I got to the front entrance of his building, Stefan's death notice had already been posted on the inside of the glass door. They'd used the same picture for it as his student ID card photo, which I knew very well.

I turned around, searching for the stranger underneath the streetlight. My eyes were still dry. But he was gone. A cat ran through the light cast by the lamp. There was nobody else on the sidewalk.

*

Mom died, too, one year later.

She'd had cancer almost throughout my entire childhood, though I hadn't realized it at the time. When I was in high school, she was admitted into the hospital a few times for surgeries that were getting more and more brutal, after which she had to wear special bras with inserts in the place of her missing breasts. The cancer eventually metastasized to her entire body, which at first disabled her physically, then started affecting her mind as well. Before she went into the hospital for the last time, she already spoke slowly and with much effort, and her eyes burned—as though she was trying with all her might to see everything she possibly could. It was insulting and degrading.

Nobody should ever have to die.

One night when I was a kid, I couldn't fall asleep, because I was afraid of slumber, which seemed to me too much like that final nonexistence that I suspected awaited all of us in the end. I lay in the darkness and gradually grew paralyzed by the thought that I would eventually have to stop thinking and stop being, wondering where I'd go and terrified that I'd actually not go anywhere.

I woke up Mom, who was sleeping in the same room, and made her promise that if something did exist in the hereafter, she'd find a way to give me a sign once she was over there. She was of course willing to promise me anything, just to comfort me. Though I think she was totally sincere.

For some reason, I still haven't received a sign from her.

After she went into the hospital for her final series of surgeries, chemotherapy, and radioactive treatments, which even the doctors no longer believed in, I went up to the rooftop of our building and lit up all the cigarettes from the pack I'd brought with me. I lined them up along the edge of a tin sheet, sat down next to them, and started taking little drags from whichever cigarette seemed like it might go out. The thin, gray plumes of smoke rose toward the blue autumn sky. I decided that if I could get all the cigarettes to burn down to their filters, without letting even a single one go out, it would all turn out to be some horrible, stupid lie.

I don't even remember if I succeeded. Maybe some wind eventually appeared and scattered them. Maybe I felt so sick that I couldn't even take just one more drag from the damn cigarettes.

Either way, Mom died.

At the funeral, I was the only one who couldn't cry. I couldn't cry for years after that. It all even seemed a little funny to me, especially when a friend of my parents' gave a speech. He was a colleague of theirs from the institute in Sliven, a celebrated bon vivant, for whom they'd invented the following rhyme: "Nasko Rachev is so swell—he wears glasses and a condom all too well." Lately, though, he'd started letting himself go and wandering around the neighborhood with a ridiculous little Bichon Frise. Mom's friends and relatives stood awkward and silent during his singsong speech about eternal fields and great beauty.

When I left Veliko Tarnovo afterward, I already knew I'd never go back again, not truly. Mom left me the apartment, which was registered under her name. But I knew I no longer had a home.

And in those years, I found that terribly exciting.

Once, when I was in elementary school, we decided to play a bizarre and extreme version of an otherwise common children's game known as Horsies, in which kids run around and give each other piggyback rides. In our version of the game, in addition to running around, the horsie-and-rider duos were supposed to also bump into one another and try to knock the other pair's rider off. Kids sometimes play such games that I often wonder how any adults exist in the world at all.

My horsie was Genady—a little thug, bully, and bad student, whom only several years later, in my capacity as the permanent, constantly reelected class president, I had to expose as such at school meetings. As a horsie, though, Genady had his advantages, and through joint efforts we managed to eventually knock down most of the other riders in the schoolyard. In the end, we were faced with the terrible twosome, consisting of Georgi "the Hose" Ivanov and Georgi "Gesha" Petkov—the former was a freakishly tall and athletic horsie with aristocratically swarthy skin that he had probably inherited from his Arab ancestors, who had galloped around the boundless Saudi deserts with sheikhs on their backs; his rider, on the other hand, had the build of an evil and supple willow and a narrow face with skewed, cold, gray eyes. I was convinced we were doomed and that was probably what brought on our downfall— right at the moment Genady made a dash toward them for our final and decisive clash, I decided to jump off his back, which caused my weight to shift and Genady to lose his balance, then trip, stagger, and fall face down, while I flew over his head and landed a few steps in front of him, at the feet of our amazed opponents, smashing my mouth on the asphalt of the Emilian Stanev Secondary School's yard.

Fortunately, most of the teeth I lost that day were still my baby teeth, so I now possess a total of twenty-eight teeth, distributed more or less evenly along my jaw. But the two front teeth I landed on were already permanent ones, so if any girl ever thought it was charming to kiss a boy with broken front teeth, I have Genady and the two Georgis to thank. (In my class, there was a third Georgi as well— Georgi "the Fatty" Georgiev. More surprisingly, through, there were also two Donikas—the gentle, blue-eyed, and fair-haired one, whose last name I no longer remember, and the sly and wild Donika Ivanova. I have no idea where that name had come from and why it disappeared so suddenly, but I never met another woman named Donika again.)

Either way, when I went home after paying a visit to the school nurse and then to the school dentist (whose league I was obviously out of, since she quickly made an appointment for me at the city's dental polyclinic, pushed me out of her office, and locked the door from the inside), I didn't have many teeth left and my face looked like a raw meatball.

My mom was terrified, but clenched her teeth and didn't even start crying.

My dad was furious. According to him, it had all been my fault. A normal kid, he said, when falling forward, instinctively stretches out both his arms in order to protect himself and break the fall, so as to be able to then simply get up and be on his way. But not our Bogdan, no, our Bogdan obviously puts his arms as far back as possible when he falls, so that he could land directly on his face and break his mug.

But we weren't going to let that happen ever again, and Dad took it upon himself to educate me on the right way to fall. To this training regimen, he applied the same pedagogical techniques he had already employed while teaching me how to swim, which had yielded brilliant results, namely—a phobia of any and all bodies of water, from the Black Sea to the bathroom tub. The coach kept a close and careful watch on the novice at all times, in order to select the most opportune moment for the next lesson. When that moment came, he would carry the lesson out quickly and decisively, in order to put the novice into the greatest possible state of shock. This was supposed to activate the novice's (i.e. my) natural mechanisms of resistance, which would then ensure the training regimen's desired effect—the body was supposed to mobilize and deal with the sudden challenge of a quickly approaching solid (or liquid) surface.

My father purposely began to trip me. Constantly. Almost every time he did, I either fell directly on my face or on my back. The only time I actually managed to stretch out my arms in order to break the fall like a normal kid, I ended up twisting my wrist.

As for my dad, he seemed to not be scared of anything.

When I was very young, he already snored with such deafening unevenness that we had him sleep in the living room, from where the thunderous sounds only reached me and my mom after being tamed by the two closed doors that stood between him and us. So the only time we had no choice but to share a room with him was during the annual family holiday to the seaside or the mountains—during those vacations, my dad always got banished to the hotel's balcony or was sent to aimlessly wander along the resort's walking paths for at least half an hour after we'd gone to bed, to give us enough time to fall asleep and not hear him when he came back and started snoring. If he fell asleep before we did, or if we had the misfortune of waking up in the middle of the night for some reason, we were done for.

But in the days when everything at home was still all right, on Saturday or Sunday mornings, Mom and I would go into the living room—still barefoot and in our pajamas—and sneak into Dad's bed. I must've been around eight. Mom and Dad then talked to each other quietly while I listened and waited for the children's morning TV show or the family ritual cleaning of the apartment to begin.

To me, Dad seemed like a large, warm, unshakable rock. It was from him that I inherited the odd physiological reflex of tearing up after a particularly wide yawn. I used to observe his large body as he lay on the bed (I never did manage to grow taller than him) and watched the tears rolling down his cheeks—like humidity dripping off a stone—and it was impossible for me to believe that he would eventually die, too. To me, it seemed as though he knew something about death that I didn't, just like he knew stuff about everything else, too, simply because he was so much bigger and smarter. I never did work up the courage to ask him about it—I could only talk to Mom about stuff like that—but the assumption itself, founded on the obvious and indisputable fact that my father didn't waste any time in fear of dying, gave me a certain confidence.

Several months after Mom died, my dad collapsed.

*

It was December 8, the national university students' holiday, and I'd gone home to wait for my first-year university friends, who were coming to visit, so we could celebrate. Veliko Tarnovo is one of those towns everyone loves to visit and spend time in—so much so, it's really a wonder that anyone ever decides to live anywhere else.

At five o'clock, it was snowing and already getting dark. My father, who at the time was running a newspaper and magazine kiosk, still wasn't home by six. On my way to pick up my friends from the train station, I went by the kiosk to see why he hadn't closed down yet.

The inside of the kiosk was dark. At the counter in the front, under the metal spring that held the newspapers in place, only a few pathetic weekly publications remained, bloated with humidity. The wind had blown some dry, icy snow into one corner of the counter. The little window, through which my dad normally handed customers their papers and people paid, was open.

The door at the back of the kiosk was also open and its inside was freezing. My father was wearing boots, a quilted jacket, and a hat with earflaps, like a bear. The small but quite powerful air heater that he used to keep warm in the winter was turned off. He was seated in an unnatural pose—his legs were tucked underneath the metal-tube chair with its dirty upholstery, his arms hung on both sides of his body in such a way that his fingers almost touched the linoleum-covered floor, and his head had fallen so far forward that it rested not on his chest but almost on his belly.

The air was icy and soaked with the sharp smell of vodka.

I tried to wake him, but Dad just kept making indistinguishable sounds and his head kept rolling forward.

I went back out, gathered up the newspapers and put away the spring, pulled down the metal window shutters, and locked them with padlocks. I was running late.

I went back in and tried to wake him up again. My father said something.

"What? Dad, I don't understand anything you're saying!"

"Leave me alone."

"I can't leave you here, you'll freeze to death or get robbed. Get up, you have to go home."

"No."

I tried to lift him. He was very heavy. When I let him sit back down into the chair, he fell asleep. I went to the phone booth across the street and called my cousin who lived in the building next door. Good, he was home. I asked him to come over to the kiosk without saying anything to Grandma and Grandpa.

It took us at least half an hour to walk the couple of blocks to our house. Dad's feet dragged in the snow, as though he was wounded. His arms kept slipping out of our grasp, which caused his entire body weight to fall either on my cousin or me. Kristian was much more patient and tactful than me, as always happens in such cases—we usually allow ourselves to be most ruthless to those who are closest to us, while the more distant someone is, the easier it is for us to be fair and polite to them.

I asked my cousin to go to the train station to pick up my university friends and take them somewhere for dinner. I stayed home with my dad, took off his boots, got him out of his quilted jacket and his ridiculous hat, and pulled a blanket over him, making sure I could actually let him sleep without having to call an ambulance.

And then my father started howling.

In February of the following year, the weather was cold and dry as a martini. A freezing wind sometimes swept down from the mountain in the evening, pierced through our clothes and turned our fingers and members into icicles, but more often the air just hung like a frozen crystal, as if trying to stay still and let the faraway yellow sun's weak rays warm us at least a little—it was as though it did all it could to stay out of the way, as much as that was possible under the laws of physics that ruled over the temperatures in the coldest month of the year.

Everybody wanted to help us. The old ladies who lived in the apartment buildings around the university and Orlov Most, where the biggest barricades were raised, came out every day at lunchtime and brought us home-made pastries and pots filled with chicken and vegetable soup. The company buses of the big fast-food chains, which the absurd historical turn of events had transformed into our temporary allies, came by regularly and supplied us with coffee and tea in plastic cups with lids. The owners of the little basement shops that looked out on the street—the kind you had to crouch down to if you wanted to buy anything— crawled out of their underground spaced and brought out dusty bottles of vodka that they passed around among us.

I remember them crushing us with their cars. As always, there were some horrible people who paid no attention to what was going on and kept trying to drive exactly through where we were standing. Even when there were dozens of other possible routes, there would always be some idiot willing to run over the symbol of his time, just to take a short-cut. So, there were some terrible moments, when we had no choice but to become a living wall, a herd of buffalo that swayed forward and pushed against the cars' metal bumpers with our knees. There were ugly scenes, when somebody in the crowd would fall to the ground and the others wouldn't be able to split up in time to avoid crushing him. There were frightening moments, when cobblestones would fly through the air—so fast and heavy, capable of knocking not just all your teeth out, but even tearing the entire bottom jaw off your face if they got you from the side.

But what I remember the most is the singing and the dancing, the embraces of strangers, and the chanting of slogans ("Anyone who doesn't jump is red trash!"). I remember sleeping with others in cocoons of four or five sleeping bags on the floors of friends who lived in the city center, because we couldn't walk all the way back to our dorms in Studentski Grad—having cut off the public transport access to it ourselves.

I remember once seeing a piano right in the middle of the main boulevard—playing it was a middle-aged man with shining eyes and wild curls in his thinning hair, while his best friends leaned against the piano decorously, and one of them turned the pages of the score.

I remember how, over a period of a few weeks, nothing mattered but the new and unfamiliar feeling that we were tempting fate and that something better was in store for us at the end of this ordeal.

Of course, now everyone thinks that we were being used; that our hot young blood was harnessed in service of the bloodless revolution. But it makes no difference whatsoever. The protests against the government were just an excuse for us to go out into the streets. Actually, it's probably us who used the protests in order to become who we are today.

Because the next time we went out into the streets, our hair would be green and our eyelids would be covered in glitter. Army trucks would crawl in front of us, loaded with thousands of watts of love power, and the DJs would rule over the elevated crowd like prophets. Compared to the revolution of the consciousness, for which we were rehearsing, the events of February 1997 were simply laughable.

The cosmos is vibrating.

At a radius of several hundred meters around the concert hall, all the glass panes of all the windows are quietly ringing in universal synchronicity. The neighborhood I live in has turned into a giant heart that has tachycardia and arrhythmia simultaneously.

When I enter the hall, at first it seems too dark. Only after slipping further in among the shadows of the dancers, I realize how deep and fascinating the contrasts are between the complete darkness, the tireless rhythm of the strobe lights, the dancing projectors, and the green lasers weaving webs though the human bodies.

Like so many others who were captivated before me, I instinctively reach out and try to touch the weightless green rays of light, which look as though they've come out of the fantasy films from my childhood.

I still don't really get the music I'm hearing. On an almost subconscious level, I take note of the things that are happening under the thunderous rhythm, which is so powerful that I'm not sure whether I'm actually perceiving it through my ears or through my feet as I stand on the shuddering floor. The stranger behind the turntables is telling a story—a monotonous race, followed by a slow and harmonious build-up of new pulsations, until they become hysterical screams of joy, accompanied by the ear-splitting whistles of the people in the hall, an astounding pause at the top of the rapture, and finally a wondrous, surprising, and wild turn, which carries the music in a completely new and yet cozily predictable direction.

I've never heard anything like it.

I've never seen so many friends embracing each other so tightly, as if that were the most natural thing in the world. I've never seen so many beautiful girls gathered in one place—girls with the glamorous dignity of princesses, girls with the mischievous energy of magical beings, girls in color, and girls whose silhouettes are barely outlined by the play of the lights.

Enormous screens hang high above our heads, projecting abstract dancing visions—computer animations and sequences from black-and-white movies and Soviet cartoons, perfect in their senselessness and playing in infinite loops. Some of the people in the hall don't even glance at them, while others can't seem to tear their eyes away.

I wonder if it might be possible to connect another computer to the screens with a word processor that would allow for words to be written, too—fairy tales, poems, free associations, which would then drift into the animated images, adding one more layer to the information flows vigorously flying around.

I'm thinking that probably everything is possible.

I'm captivated by the people who are wandering around or dancing, as if they were lost in a dream, as if they were aliens, or elves; I'm fascinated by the unfamiliar glint in their eyes, by their wide and gentle smiles, by their bright-colored clothes, and by their movements, simultaneously smooth and quick, as if they were floating in their own element in the silvery darkness, feeding on and riding the swift currents of the music. In amazement, I watch them discovering one another, as though the chemical compounds in their blood, still unknown to me, had drawn halos over their heads, like identification signs which are helping them locate one another across the enormous, echoing hall and among the hundreds and hundreds of other bodies in it.

And then—at the dawn of time, so far back in the past

that by now it all seems like a magical, innocent legend told by somebody else—long before the warm stickiness of another ecstasy pill, before the uncompromising, sharp, buzzing energy of the amphetamines, and even before that barely noticeable warmth and the total mussing up of the hair, made wet from all the dancing and the water guns, which would be brought on by over-the-counter ephedrine mixed with Coke—back then, at that first party, I felt with all my senses that magic moment in which the whole world changed and nothing was ever going to be the same.

And as I walked home in the morning, I heard for the first time that soft but persistent ringing in my ears, which I would get very friendly with before long; and I felt for the first time that sweet lead in my legs, which dancing for eight or nine hours straight would pour into them every weekend; and I saw for the first time the guys and girls waiting at the bus stops, hiding behind their sunglasses with their hair dye running from the heat—they were lost in the regular world of daylight, where other people were going to work just as they were coming home from a party; and I already knew that I wanted to be a part of this new world.

My life could finally begin.

À L'OMBRE
DES JEUNES FILLES
EN FLEURS

to the girls: thank you for everything

3.1

Once upon a time, there was a small town at the foot of some tall blue mountains.

Sometimes the mountains blended in with the blue of the sky, while other times their sharp outline stood out against it, and a furious cold wind descended from them, but the sea was so close that the people from the town often heard the sound of the waves in their dreams, so during the summer they took the train and went to the beach every weekend.

One spring day, a girl was at home on the top floor of a tall high-rise apartment building in the town's outskirts, while a sad young actor from the local theater stood outside her front door and threatened to kill himself.

Frankly speaking, the girl wasn't all that worried about it. She possessed the gift of such splendid beauty that she had grown accustomed to boys from her school and even to other, older men behaving oddly in her presence. This particular actor had spent months insisting on getting something—anything—from her, but the more he begged, the less attention she paid to him. She was nineteen, but she already knew that once it got to the point of a man having to beg for something—be it help, mercy, or love—it would be to everyone's benefit that he never get it.

But on that day, things were a little different. This time, the sad young actor had brought a gun with him, which he waved around theatrically on one side of the door, while the girl observed him through the peephole on the other, and ignored his pleas to at least open up. The girl thought about calling the police, but two considerations of a fundamentally different nature stopped her: the selfish distrust that the young actor was capable of such a decisive step, which naturally gave rise to the very valid assumption that the gun, most likely a stolen theater prop, wasn't loaded; and the altruistic conviction that if the local police guys caught the deranged young actor waving a gun around in front of her door, this would put an even more tragic end to his life by sending him to prison or the local mental asylum.

One way or another, the girl was sincerely taken aback when the actor finally put the gun to his temple, pulled the trigger, and blew his skull to pieces.

Through the peephole, she watched as the young actor's head, with his expressive sad eyes and his dramatic, messy hair, suddenly flung to the left, slammed into his shoulder, then bounced back with such force that it slammed into his right shoulder—then blood and brains spilled out of the wide, jagged-edged hole, which opened up on the other side of his skull.

The stairwell of the high-rise apartment building, where the girl lived with her parents in a small apartment on the top floor, shook with a deafening rumble.

The young actor lay sprawled out across the landing and never stirred again. Several seconds passed. Doors began to open on the lower floors.

"Pff," Dena said.

When she finally got tired of having to answer the same questions over and over again and to wear sunglasses whenever she came out of the house, because the people in the small town kept pointing a finger at her while worriedly whispering to each other, Dena decided to pack her bags and leave. An even bigger journey awaited her at the end of the summer anyway, so she thought she might as well do a dress rehearsal for it. For a while now, she had been chatting with some people online—they were all living together in a big apartment in the big city, where at least twelve people were sleeping at any given time, while another twelve could not fall asleep for anything in the world. Dena asked if they'd mind if she joined them, they said they wouldn't, and on one particularly hot day at the beginning of the summer, she showed up at their front door.

The apartment was located on the top floor of the tallest high-rise building in a suburb at the edge of the big city and it really was legendary. It had no furniture, apart from a dozen identical low mattresses, on which people slept, couldn't sleep, just lay, sat, jumped, made love, chatted, smoked all kinds of stuff, took pictures, played Scrabble, drank coffee, browsed through magazines, read books, and watched movies. The apartment only had three books in it, and they were all reference books: *Cinema 1896–1996*, *Substance Abuse*, and *The Complete Encyclopedia of Sneakers*. There was also just one videotape, which had been rented from the local video rental store once, but so long ago that none of the original event's witnesses lived in the apartment anymore, and nobody dared to either try to return the tape, or rent a new one. This is why the people in the apartment watched *The Matrix* every single night and knew all the lines by heart.

When Dena got to the apartment on the top floor (the apartment building was so tall that people often fell asleep in the elevator while waiting for it to climb all the way up), the front door was already open, and a girl stood at the threshold, waiting to give Dena a hug. Out of the apartment's current tenants, the girl had lived there the longest, having moved in after the housing board kicked her out of her previous place. (Her previous place was an attic. After she had first moved in, the neighbors figured she was doing some renovations, which seemed to be taking place throughout the day and night. Initially, they were quite understanding, since they assumed the new tenant was trying to get better set up, but after the renovations continued in full swing for more than a few weeks, they finally decided to ring her doorbell and ask how things were going and whether she might need anything. She opened the door in her pajamas, blinking confusedly. No renovations were taking place. The girl had been merely listening to Scandinavian techno nonstop.)

Dena walked into the first room of the apartment and saw another girl standing in front of the mirror and covering her face with glitter. The girl turned to Dena, gave her an anxious smile, and said:

"Welcome. You're not going to disappear now, are you?"

(The girl had come from a regular family in a town by the sea, which had suddenly become wealthier than they could imagine even in their wildest dreams. One day, some bad people had kidnapped her father and held him for ransom, but the negotiations had gone haywire, and he was never heard from again. Since then, the girl had developed a phobia that the people around her—relatives, friends, lovers—could disappear at any moment.)

Dena reassured her that she was going to stick around for a few months at least, and went over to the apartment's second room, where some guys and girls were sitting in a circle on the mattresses and smoking a joint with pointed concentration. It was immediately obvious that they were no amateurs—they looked like people who hadn't slept in at least two days; their enormous eyes were shining, their smiles looked crazy, and they all kept mysteriously silent. But every once in a while, one of them would say something wise and the others would nod their heads in agreement. (For example, right before Dena left the room, one of the guys said: "You come up with stuff when you take a blotter, then you make it on speed, and get high to listen to it."

Dena went over to the third room and paused at the threshold. The room had no furniture—not even a mattress—and all four of its walls were covered in maps, sketches, and unprofessional black-and-white photographs of local landmarks, sections of parks and gardens, shopping centers, fast-food joints, cafés, bars, and dance clubs. There was a picture of a train in a station, as well as a close-up of a bench, where somebody had carved some initials inside a heart and linked by a plus sign. The photographs were strategically placed all over the map printouts, and connected by arrows and mysterious symbols drawn in black marker. Several locations were circled or underlined with a sweep, some of them more than once, while others were ominously crossed out. All in all, the room looked like the lair of one of those mass murderers or terrorists from the movies. As she walked around and examined the photographs and the maps on the walls, Dena regretted not having a flashlight, with which to cast dramatic lights and shadows on them.

(Between you and me, what she imagined wasn't that far off from reality. The guy who lived in that room was trying to destroy the memory of his lost love. A few years earlier, the guy he'd loved more than anything in the world had gone to the States on a summer work-and-travel program, then stayed on to study for a year, and in the end had moved in with an aging literature professor. The guy who remained behind in Bulgaria couldn't bear to see the evidence of his lover's absence every day—all the places where they'd once walked, where their fingers had accidentally brushed against one another, where they'd kissed, tried on clothes, eaten dinner, drank coffee, danced, and kissed. That's why he came up with a systematic plan to destroy all the pieces of evidence one by one.)

The fourth room of the apartment was the kitchen. Since nobody ever went in there to eat, a girl was using it as a hiding spot to study for her exams. Dena wished her good luck and continued on.

Sitting in the fifth room, there were two fifteen- or sixteen-year-old guys and an older man. The young guys watched the man in awe and absorbed his each and every word with their mouths open. And it couldn't be any other way—the man was Barabas, the legendary techno DJ, the Dionysius of tribal bacchanals and the Apostle of music, who'd been touring around the country for years, stopping even in the tiniest small towns in the outskirts of the Balkan Mountains, where he single-handedly organized parties and revolutionary committees, sold his own records at symbolic prices to beginner DJs, initiated his followers into the secrets of the fader and the mixing of alternative time signatures, and in this way saved hundreds of guys and girls every year—maybe not exactly from drugs and all the other dangers of the big city and the revolution, but surely from their dull life and daily grind, from the lack of emotion, hope, and stories worth telling. When he saw Dena, Barabas smiled at her kindly and nodded in the direction of the last room, from where music could be heard.

The music coming from the last room did not resemble anything Dena had ever heard before. If we assume that

the deafening dry bang of the shot in front of her parents'
small-town apartment's door had been the most unpleasant
sound ever to have reached her ears, then the music in the
big-city apartment's last room was exactly the opposite. It
was rather quiet and soft (although it carried the promise
of strength and enough decibels to shake up a crowd of
thousands), it was warm, juicy, and almost organic in its
pulsations, it was as sophisticated and multilayered as a sym-
phony and as simple as love. It was so expressive and vibrant
that it made even the inanimate objects smile and fill up
with rhythm to the point where one had to ask oneself
whether such a thing as "inanimate objects" existed at all.

Dena held her breath and entered the room.

A guy was squatting by the turntables, pressing one
headphone up to his ear with his shoulder and using his
swift gnarled fingers to flip through the records in his
beat-up case as he searched for the next track for his mix.
He lifted his green eyes toward her. His skinny, wiry right
arm had a faded lightning bolt tattoo on it, partly concealed by his t-shirt sleeve.

Calmly, Dena looked him in the eyes. His gaze darted
down her body, then momentarily went back to his turntables and records, and finally relaxed on her eyes.

"I'm Bobby," the guy said. "And if you don't leave this
room within the next minute, I'm going to start kissing
you."

"I'm Dena," the girl said.

She then went up to the window, looked outside, and
tapped her fingers on the windowsill to the rhythm of the

music, which was gaining momentum underneath the guy's fingers, then she smiled and turned back around to face him:

"How are you?"

*

The summer of their love was short and so hot that the tram tracks got warped from the heat and led the trams to unknown destinations. Dena and Bobby were doing everything the other way around: they started living in the big city just as its regular inhabitants were leaving on holiday to the seaside; what mattered to the two of them weren't the days from Monday through Friday, but the weekends; they used the public transport to go home in the morning, right when normal people were using it to go to work. Together with others like them, Dena and Bobby zealously kept frequenting the same clubs, where they kept jumping up and down in the same spot like Shaolin monks, until the symmetrical imprints of their soles were visible in the ground beneath their feet. Their nights were filled with a piercing light, the rain washed their hot faces, and their whistles shrieked up to the sky.

Dena and Bobby loved each other so much that when they made love, it was as if they were the protagonists in an American blockbuster—there was an exposition, a rising tension, a thrill, action, romance, comic relief, a plot twist, an explosive climax, and finally an open ending that lent itself to a sequel.

But then everything came to an end.

One morning, Dena got on a bus and left.

Nothing in the world could prepare them for this moment. Other separations tend to have an element of ominous fatality about them, and this seems to lessen the strength of their sadness by the very fact of their inevitability. But when Bobby saw the bus doors close and watched as Dena waved at him from the inside with a brave smile on her face, then covered her ears with her headphones, something in him broke forever. It was neither the first nor the last time somebody would leave him.

But this time, it hurt like hell.

When Dena left, all the land languished and suffered from her absence. The rulers of the big city were getting replaced more and more quickly and senselessly, and the new ones were growing stupider and crueler than those who came before them. Riots erupted on the streets. The electronic revolution, in which Bobby followed his guru Barabas, entered a darker and sharper phase. Everything they did—whether it had to do with music, dancing, love, experimenting with drugs, or their relationship to the authorities—now had an element of risk and revenge to it. For their part, the rulers kept passing new laws against the free people, which branded them as criminals, while the real criminals remained at large in their flashy cars as big as fortresses.

The dangerous charm of leaving was getting more and more tempting. Every day, hundreds, even thousands of young people were getting on trains, buses, and airplanes, and leaving their homeland. Most of them never came back. It was said that they'd found a new life somewhere over there, beyond the borders, but the proof of that was so sketchy and illusory that those who stayed behind preferred to abandon all hope of ever seeing them again. The few who did come back were changed to the point of seeming like different people altogether, or like some artificial shells with which the foreign lands' inhabitants had replaced the erstwhile friends and loved ones.

Bobby's music was becoming more and more desperate. When he spun records at parties, nobody ever danced to them anymore. Instead, the music he played made everyone retreat into the darkest corners and stare ahead into the empty space, robbed of the will to live. Nothing seemed to help. Nothing seemed to matter. Every night, at the exact same time, his heart convulsed with such sharp pain that he wasn't sure he'd make it to the morning.

So, one evening Bobby also got on a bus and left.

His plan was simple and brazen to the point of insanity. He was about to do something no mortal had ever done before. He was going to go across the border without forgetting who he was, where he'd come from, and why he'd left; he was going to find Dena at the other end of the continent, where nothing was what it seemed; he was going to make her remember him and their love, and he was going to get her to come back with him.

He was going to get her back from the foreign land.

*

The bus traveled for three days and three nights, crossing unfamiliar lands and taking Bobby further and further away from the places he knew, the languages he understood, and the faces that seemed to him like faces of his own kind. By the time he finally arrived in the small town where Dena was living, everything had become utterly unfamiliar. At first, he didn't even recognize her—standing under the eaves of the bus station, she was hiding from the cool pouring rain, while her hair and ears, which he'd loved so much, were hidden under the hood of some new and strange piece of clothing he was also seeing for the first time.

In the small town at the end of the world, the nights were longer and darker because it was located much further to the north than their homeland, but the streets were cleaner and more brightly lit, and the people who roamed them looked more alive somehow—as if they were all headed somewhere that promised to be very interesting. While they walked down the street, Dena often greeted different people in their throaty native tongue, and once stopped and spoke to some guy for a long time—the two of them kept laughing and repeating the same name over and over again, which Bobby had never heard before. The only word he recognized was the word "party," but almost all its sounds were pronounced differently in the local language, so it left a totally different taste in one's mouth.

(On the first night, though, Bobby and Dena didn't go to any party. They went to her place, which was in a working-class neighborhood close to the university and had a window that looked out on the rail line, and Bobby took a shower while Dena prepared dinner, consisting of pasta and sauces, and meat and vegetables, which he was also seeing for the first time. Their taste was unfamiliar, but quite pleasant. After that, the two of them sat at the table in the small kitchen silently, while the candles between them burned low. When they finally burned out, it became completely dark, and Dena's eyes, which until that moment had shined together with the flames, also died down. The air seemed to have grown heavier. When Bobby was finally able to overcome his suffocating laziness, he got up and took Dena by the hand, and her hand was heavier and limper than he remembered. She also got up and led him to the bed. Only then—after they took their clothes off and embraced each other—did the life return to their bodies, and they started embracing more tightly, then hesitantly kissed, as if they were doing it for the first time, like back in that faraway room, and only then did their desire return, and they could finally become the same Dena and Bobby that they'd each known and loved.)

On the second day, the rain stopped but the sky remained gray and dark, and by the early afternoon the small town's yellow streetlights were already turned on and flickering. Dena had to go to her job in an African restaurant and let Bobby use her bike to ride around and explore the town. He liked getting around by bike. All of the small town's streets, sidewalks, and pathways had lines on them, designating which lane was for cars, which was for people, and which was for bikes, and everyone obeyed them. It was cool and humid, but Dena had given him a hat, a scarf, and a pair of gloves, so Bobby rode the bike around for a long time—so long that he ended up getting lost. He then stopped another guy on a bike and somehow managed to explain that he was trying to find his way to the university. The other guy smiled and gestured to Bobby to follow him, then got on his bike and rode off while Bobby trailed him. When they reached the university and Bobby started recognizing some streets, the other guy waved goodbye and vanished into the darkness, while Bobby felt pleased, and laughed—for the first time since he'd arrived.

(And on the second night, while they looked through the free magazine at the listings of all the cinemas, the theatres, the galleries, the concert halls, the bars and restaurants, the converted warehouses and factories, the illegal neighborhoods, and the apartments that you needed a password to enter, the bomb shelters and the abandoned subway lines now turned into dance clubs, it seemed to him that, in this small town at the end of the world, all the musicians he'd ever wanted to hear perform live were playing, and all the films were screening, and all the plays were staged, and all the cocktails were served, and nothing ever ran out, as if he were in some magical land beyond the real world's borders.)

On the third day, the sun rose bright and pure in the pale blue sky, its rays shining over the sharp-edged gothic roofs of the tall buildings in the center and over the cathedrals' bell towers, which shot up like spikes. The narrow pedestrian streets filled with crowds of beautiful, well-dressed, smiling, and polite people who seemed to know something more about life and managed to fill each and every minute of it with pleasure and meaning. When the bank employees had a glass of wine at one of the sidewalk bistros during their lunch break, their laughter sounded more sincere and contagious than the laughter of all the artists in Dena and Bobby's homeland, who only pretended to be free. When the chubby shopkeepers in the off-the-rack clothing stores left work at the end of the day, they walked among their hometown's antique buildings like princesses. When Bobby and Dena stepped onto the crosswalk, all the flashy cars on the street, as big and inaccessible as fortresses, came to a halt and waited for them to cross, while their semi-transparent windshields revealed pink smiling faces.

(That evening, Dena took Bobby to the interior court-yard of a modern art museum, where surprisingly comfortable concrete benches in abstract shapes were scattered, on which young, pleasant, and open people sat drinking beer from plastic cups. The two of them accidentally ran into some people they knew from past parties in their home-land's big city, from back when they were living together in that apartment. While speaking to them and to their new friends who didn't know Bulgarian, Bobby suddenly discovered that he'd started to understand some of the words in the new language. He sat quietly and sipped his beer for a while, then finally decided to follow the realization's thread and see where it led.

He was starting to feel at home.

He was starting to forget why he'd come.)

On the fourth day, the two of them sat in a café on the banks of the river, which had a view of the large gray city hall. The sun gleamed on the ripples of the river, which were as heavy as lead.

"Come to me," Bobby said.

Dena was silent.

"I don't want us to lose each other just like that," he went on. "I don't want to go and leave you here, because next time you come back, we'll be different, and there's a chance, no matter how small, that we won't love each other anymore. I don't want to take that chance. Come back to me."

"What will I do there?" she asked.

"What will you do here?" he asked. "What is there to do anyway? Love is the most important thing. If we lose it now, we can't be sure it'll ever happen to us again."

Dena fell silent again. Then she smiled to herself and said:

"If I came back, I'd be the first to ever do that. We'd be rewriting history."

"I know," Bobby replied. "But it's not impossible."

"Why don't you come here?"

"What would I do here?" he asked.

Dena stared at him, then put her cup down and stood up.

"I'm going to work. I'll see you tonight."

On the fifth day, it was late at night and the two of them were in Dena's apartment. The windows rattled softly every time a train passed on the tracks below. The bed was so high up that they had to climb a little ladder to reach it, and while Dena was on top of Bobby, she lifted her arms, pushed her palms against the ceiling, and pressed herself against him more tightly. It felt great, of course, but Bobby thought to himself that the only way she would know that trick was if she'd already made love to somebody else in that bed, and that thought made him feel so miserable that he shared it with her. Dena's eyes shone in the dark and she told him that he was also doing things to her that he hadn't done before—things that were more numerous and different than the thing with the ceiling. Then they both fell silent and lay next to each other for a long time, staring straight ahead. They didn't embrace—they lay on their backs, and only their shoulders touched.

"I'll come," Dena finally said. "I'll come back to you. I'll change my entire life around. But you have to give me something equally big in return."

"Okay," Bobby said.

"You have to quit messing around with other girls," she said. "If I come back now, I'd be doing it because I believe I can spend my whole life with you. And only with you."

"Okay," he repeated.

"I won't set any other conditions," she went on. "I don't care where we live, what we do for a living, or how much money we have. You said it and I believe you: love is the most important thing. But you have to understand something very important, too, and you have to agree to it before I move back. If you ever as much as look at another girl the way you look at me, you'll never see me again."

"Okay," Bobby said for the third time in a row.

On the last night, Dena took Bobby to her favorite dance club in the foreign land. She felt connected to the place by so many memories, some of which Bobby wasn't supposed to find out about under any circumstances, that at first she felt hesitant about going. But she wanted to show him something she knew he'd never seen before, and also to say goodbye to the place herself.

And the place really was like nothing he'd ever seen before. If we assume that the other dance club, which at that moment was impatiently awaiting its terrible fate— that other dance club with the piercing, scraping noise of torn metal pillars, the menacing wet cracking sound of broken bones, and the desperate screams of children get- ting crushed underneath the pillars, that place we never talk about, that place we will never forget—if we assume that was the most terrible place Bobby could ever end up, then Dena's favorite dance club in the foreign land was exactly the opposite.

This club started out on the rooftop of a factory's aban- doned dining hall in the town's industrial part and continued downward, in a dizzyingly winding series of levels, terraces, and halls, toward an underground labyrinth of passageways and doors, which were shaped like round submarine doors and didn't always lead to where the laws of physics dictated they should. The club offered so many different kinds of music and so many different kinds of delights that it looked like heaven—or at least how Bobby imagined heaven to look like. While Dena held his hand and took him on a tour around the club, which she knew well by now, he didn't even try to memorize which way they were going and just looked around with wide-open and shining eyes. From time to time, she turned to look at him and smiled proudly.

Later that night, the two of them split up for a while, but Bobby had already taken some unfamiliar magical pill and felt supernaturally certain he'd be able to find her, regardless of where in that whole tangled place she might be located, as if she had a halo or a beacon over her head that only he could see. When he got thirsty, Bobby found a bar and ordered a sparkling mineral water. After the first sip, he realized he had asked for the water in the foreign land's language, without even giving it a thought. It was as though the words, generated by his thirst, had formed inside his consciousness on their own, and by the time they reached his lips, they were already clad in the unfamiliar language's sounds.

Bobby laughed, turned around, and spotted a smiling girl who stood in the cone of light cast down by a fantastical lamp. The girl was slight, and had little short and slightly crooked legs, which at that moment seemed to him very cute. Right in the instant when he took a step toward her, a quiet scream sounded inside the base of his head, which seemed like a warning, but its words were in Bobby's native language and he didn't understand them. He walked up to the girl and stood next to her, smiling the whole time. She smiled back at him and pointed to the tattoo on his right arm, which peeked out from underneath his t-shirt sleeve.

"Can I see it?"

"Not really," Bobby replied and lifted his sleeve a little,

enough for her to see that the black lightning bolt extended toward his shoulder. "It goes all the way up and across my back, then reaches my other shoulder. I can't show it to you unless I undress."

The girl smiled a little wider.

"This is a trap," she said.

Bobby smiled, too, even more widely, and took a sip from the carbonated water, which gave off sparks in his mouth.

"That's right," he replied. "A trap countless adolescent girls have already fallen into."

The girl laughed.

"I'm not an adolescent girl."

"I'm happy to hear that," Bobby said, then did something very strange.

Just as he was about to extend his hand for a handshake, the girl's skin started to glow with a strange kind of light, and he decided it would be much more appropriate for him to kiss her on the neck. As soon as he did, she giggled.

Dena was watching him from the other end of the bar.

In the first instant, Bobby didn't even stop smiling, since he didn't feel like he'd done anything wrong.

He took a step toward her.

Dena turned around and vanished into the shadows.

He looked over his shoulder.

The girl was gone from underneath the lamp, too.

The supernatural feeling about the beacon over Dena's head, which was supposed to help him locate her regardless of where she was, abruptly vanished—as if somebody had turned the water valve off in the shower. Bobby hesitantly walked to where he'd last seen Dena, but he found no trace of her. He opened one of the round metal doors (which was much heavier than all the other doors he had opened that night), but found himself in a completely unfamiliar space without any music, where it was almost completely dark, and where pale people wandered around without talking or smiling. Bobby kept opening more and more doors, climbing up and going down, and searched around the dance club's entire labyrinth, all the way from the rooftop to the underground spaces, but it felt as if he was doomed to go through the same rooms over and over again, while never reaching others.

It was already morning, there was nobody else left in the club, and Bobby was almost falling over with exhaustion, when he finally remembered Dena's last words to him, and it dawned on him that he would never see her again.

While traveling back to his native land and its big city, which was going to indifferently take him back into its anonymous embrace, he felt as though he were crossing the land of the dead. The bus flew past gray and mournful fields, tormented by poverty and hunger, and the horizon was so flat that it seemed like the bus had stopped and wasn't moving for hours.

When he returned to the big city, Bobby threw himself into the nocturnal whirlwind with such fury and soon sank so deeply into it, that there was no hope of him ever floating back up to the surface, where the days mattered and where the meaning of life didn't get measured in numbers—numbers that stood for grams, hours, or times he got laid.

His music became so hard to listen to that even his own friends stopped coming to his parties, and when his former fans blew as hard as they could on their whistles, it wasn't with admiration, but with disgust and the desire to silence him. So Bobby quit making music, but didn't quit everything else.

And it was all leading up to that one particular black night, when Bobby wound up in that one particular dance club at that one particular time and found himself among that one particular crowd, when the metal pillars succumbed under the dancing kids' weight and the whole structure mercilessly collapsed on top of the kids below. Some say that as he lay there, right in the middle of the mush of metal, concrete, and human flesh, and bright red blood gushed out of his crushed lungs with a wheezing sound, Bobby looked straight up with wide-open and frightened eyes and kept saying the same three German words over and over again.

Komm. Zu. Mir.

Others, though, tell a different story.

They say that six months, a year, or maybe three years later, Bobby was finally able to disentangle himself from the sinister whirlwind of drugs and the artificial love of girls with dilated pupils and glitter on their eyelids, and never touched his records again, so that on that particular black night, he was actually home and having a slightly tipsy phone conversation with a friend.

Some even say that he continued waiting for her return. And that a few years later, Dena came back after all—even though it was only for the summer—and the two of them hesitated for a moment, but then embraced each other again, and she came back the following summer, too.

And so, they lived happily ever after—with Dena spending nine months out of the year in the foreign land and three months in their native land, which Bobby never left again. In that sense, they were more or less happy—at least most of the time.

And that was already much more than anyone had any right to hope for.

3.2

this summer's candy is pink and has dolphins on it.
in the evening the apartment gathers
the usual suspects
vera, who lives there now,
after the housing board threw her out
of her previous place
bobby, who maybe lives there too,
judging from his turntables and records
in the last room
teddy, who's a friend of bobby's
ekaterina, teddy's girlfriend
bozhana, bobby's "girlfriend"
because everyone knows that bobby's real girlfriend is
in germany
probably everyone but him
and maybe twelve other people, each of whom
knows at least one of the others
but there's always one or two strangers, too

so it never gets boring.
later
when the lines soften and the light
becomes muted on its own,
and halos blossom around the objects
bobby takes bozhana by the hand and leads her outside,
and two of them observe everything around them
with wide-open, dark eyes
and with that childish amazement
that makes up roughly thirty-five percent of the motivation
to keep doing it over and over again.
the place is nearby and—after all it's the end of the '90s,
so the very fabric of existence is soaked with irony—it is
called
ecstasy.
when they go in, the bouncer looks at them in amazement,
which almost turns into a reflection of their own:
a guy of an indeterminate age between twenty and
twenty-five
and a pretty girl of twenty,
who has no business here,
unless her business was to work here.
the guy asks for one particular girl
that he knows well
then the three of them go into a room,
where there is nothing but a large, clean bed
the guy and the girl who works here
take their clothes off right away,
then together they undress bozhana,

who looks at them with dilated pupils
and a calm smile
bobby and bozhana are so high
that even the drops of sweat glistening on their skin
are like chemical pearls
their gentle excitement
magically transfers to the girl who works here
and for the next two hours she forgets she's working
so when they embrace and caress and kiss and lick and
suck and penetrate one another
the three of them are making love.
when bobby and bozhana go back to the apartment
bobby pulls teddy into the kitchen and tells him
what he's just done
teddy is impressed.
do you know why you feel like fucking so badly
whenever you get this fucked up?
because your body can feel that the end is near,
and it tries at least to reproduce itself
that's why, even though you can't eat or sleep
and sometimes you don't even have the energy to talk
you can still fuck all day long.

in the morning everyone comes home together
from another place, called
deep down.
well, not quite everyone
ekaterina and teddy stayed behind in the apartment
and when they ran out of cigarettes,

they went out to buy some and didn't get back
by the time the others went out
and not exactly together either
because in the club bobby gets captivated by a girl
in a little pink top with thin straps
and talks to her for two and a half hours
and when he finally leans over
to kiss her on the neck
she smiles understandingly
but tells him that she's the DJ's girlfriend
and that she thought he knew
and bozhana decides to leave on her own.
so on their way back to the apartment
bobby talks to some guy he doesn't know
he has bright red, matted hair, and walks with them
and they're talking about ecstasy
and bobby tells him
look, i'm not planning to do this for the rest of my life
i'm only going to go to parties until i'm like, thirty-two
and the guy gets offended and laughs
how exactly did you set that as the upper limit?
bobby looks at him confused
in the bright light of the morning, which streams in even
through their dark sunglasses
and the guy says
take me, for example, i'm thirty-four.

at around eight thirty. bobby and vera are drinking instant
coffee.

vera manages to look beautiful and clean
even in the morning.
they sometimes hold hands
though they have an unspoken agreement that they won't
sleep together ever again
after having had sex exactly 3.3 minutes
since their first encounter
then deciding that they would actually really like
to become friends and
then vera comes up with a genius plan
now listen carefully
our birthdays are on the same day, right?
i just came up with the perfect idea for a party:
i invite twelve of my ex-boyfriends,
lovers, or friends that i've already had sex with,
and then six more guys that i'd like
to have sex with but still haven't
you also invite twelve of your ex-girlfriends,
lovers, or friends that you've had sex with,
and then six more girls that you'd like to have sex with,
but still haven't
since you and i are friends
and we've had sex
we're obviously each other's type
therefore it's very likely
that many of the people we invite
would also be into one another
we'll have the birthday party right here in the apartment
and we'll only set out a bottle of mineral water and one

glass bowl in the middle of the living room,
filled with pink dolphins.
how does that sound?
bobby's mind is blown
it sounds like
the best party on earth.

at that exact moment the doorbell rings.
vera lights a cigarette before she opens it
then exhales the smoke with relief
when instead of the entire housing board
she sees it's only a young man standing at the threshold.
the guy has longish black hair
and his eyes are very dark
vera's eyes are light, but right at that moment
her pupils are so dilated
that they look black as well
and the two of them look into each other's eyes for a while.
but the guy is wearing a suit and tie and pointing
to the lock outside the door
where a set of keys is swinging lightly
on a panda keychain
he comes from the mirror world, where people get up in
the morning
and go to work, dressed in suits
and do not forget their keys in the door.
thank you
vera says.
you're welcome

he says and lights a cigarette, too
i live right below you.
vera says
oh, yeah?
he says
yeah.
and why are you dressed like that?
because i'm headed to an exam, dear girl.
"dear girl"?
uh-huh
i'm a future lawyer and, even though this is obviously not
a very good moment to go into such kinds of topics, lately
i've been participating in the establishment of bulgaria's
future middle class, by methodically trying to become a
little screw in the system and performing the things that
society and economics expect of me under the given historical circumstances.
the guy has somehow managed to come in and close
the door behind him
most of the others look at him as if he were an alien
or as if they were aliens
depending on the point of view.
and what if the given historical circumstances were
different?
i'd be doing something different
the guy answers with no hesitation
then launches into an extensive treatment of the power
structure
in the elven kingdoms, where

the monarchy gets passed down by inheritance, but since
the monarchs like all the other elves are practically
immortal, it practically never gets passed down, and so on.
most of the people in the apartment
are starting to get distracted
their concentration rarely stretches beyond
the specifics of the moment:
the music, the changed states of consciousness, love
this is their blessing
and their curse.
but bobby looks at him with interest
and vera looks at him with dilated pupils
and hands him the joint she's just rolled
the guy smokes in a funny way
and vera asks what his name is
the guy gives them a mocking, but compassionate look
with his very dark eyes
and tells them his real name
but quickly adds that people usually call him
charlie.
and why are you looking at us like this? bobby asks.
like what? charlie says.
with a mocking, but compassionate look, bobby says.
charlie looks at him a little more carefully
and says:
because i think an interesting story
is going to come out of this place.
and then vera winks at bobby
and invites charlie to her birthday party.

3.3

It was the hot yellow summer of 1999 and I couldn't come.

I hadn't come inside a woman since returning from Germany two months earlier. I masturbated regularly, but whenever I went to bed with a woman, I was always so high on ecstasy and cheap amphetamines that I always got a more or less certain erection, but could never actually come. I'd fuck them harder and harder, and faster and faster, I'd put their bodies into positions that looked more and more pornographic, my face would turn red from all the effort and sweat would run down my chest, but it was like I was fucking them with a piece of wood. In the end, I'd either give up or the women would make it clear that they wouldn't mind if I stopped. I think they enjoyed it, most of the time—at least at the beginning and in the middle.

So the last woman I'd come inside of was still Dena.

I had a month left before the start of my mandatory military service when Teddy called me on the phone.

"Do you feel like going to an open-air party in Varna?"

he asked. "I have free passes."

"How would we get there?"

"By car. I can ask Koki to give us a ride."

"Yeah, but then we'll have to take him to the party with us."

"Not necessarily," Teddy said. "He's got some friends in Varna, so he'll probably go out with them and get so trashed that he'll have to go home and go to bed."

"Is Ekaterina coming?"

Ekaterina was Teddy's girlfriend, and she really got on my nerves.

"No," Teddy said and I could hear him grinning even through the receiver. "Ekaterina is studying for her exams."

"Great," I said. "When do we leave?"

While Koki drove one hundred sixty kilometers per hour down the highway just before Varna, the sky started getting darker more and more quickly. The nights were already becoming shorter, but it wasn't that noticeable yet. Teddy and I were both wearing sunglasses.

"So, are you two going to get laid at this party, or what?" Koki asked.

"Doubt it," Teddy said and humbly waved his hand.

Koki turned to face me in the backseat, without slowing down. The car smoothly bounced over the highway's potholes, like a motorboat bouncing over the waves.

"This guy here," he said and pointed his sausage of a finger at Teddy. "You can take him to Mars and he'd still find something to fuck, even if it's a snake."

The party was on the beach and went on until morning.

Teddy and I got so high that we somehow missed the entire set of the world-famous DJ we'd actually come to see. The blinding sun rose over the sea, climbing higher and higher. There was something unseemly about the deafening booming of the bass, which echoed over the white sand and the water's calm surface. Just on the other side of the fence, some elderly people were already laying down their towels on the sand, and casting suspicious glances in our direction. About one hundred scraggy people with toothy grins and enormous sunglasses like insect eyes were still roaming around at the party.

I left Teddy sitting in the shade of the speakers and sucking on a Bacardi Breezer, and took off with a girl from Varna, whom I'd gone home with the last time I was there.

"Where do you live?"

"You don't remember?" she smiled underneath her sunglasses. "Really close to here."

"What are you on?"

She told me. The list was quite long.

"What do you want to do now?" I asked.

"We'll freshen up, get some rest. Then we can go out and have some coffee. Or we can come back to the after-party."

Her place was cool and quiet. The curtains were closed. We took our sunglasses off. In the semi-darkness, everything appeared a little blurry.

We showered and went to bed. There were two single beds in the room, placed at a right angle with each other. The other bed was empty.

We started kissing and I got hard. We got into the 69

position, the girl opened her legs, and I started licking her while she grabbed my dick and put it in her mouth. We were at it for a long time, things got heated, and she came. I didn't. A while later, the girl's roommate came home, but we'd heard her turning the key in the door, so by the time she came into the room and lay down in the other bed, we had returned to a more decent position, with both our heads on the pillow and our eyes closed. We lay there and listened to the roommate's steady breathing.

"I want some more," I whispered.

"I do, too," the girl from Varna smiled lazily.

"We could try and do it very quietly," I suggested.

"Not that quietly. She'll have to get up for work soon."

My heart was beating really fast and hard.

"Or we could wake her up as well," I suggested. "Do you want to?"

The girl from Varna smiled again.

"Yes."

I got out of bed and crouched by the roommate's bed. Then I leaned over and started softly kissing her forehead, her eyes, her lips, and her ears. She slowly opened her eyes, smiled sleepily, and looked at the girl in the other bed, then at me. The girl in the other bed half rose and leaned on her elbow, then started caressing her roommate's hair while looking her in the eyes and smiling calmly. I continued kissing her and she started kissing me back. Our tongues touched for the first time.

"Hey," she said in pretend reproach. "What are you two up to?"

The two of them started kissing and I went down between the roommate's thighs and licked her for a while. Afterward, I climbed back up, kissed the first girl, and slipped inside the roommate. We were at it for a while, but I couldn't come and it eventually became too hot to carry on.

"Let me get some rest," the roommate said. "You hopped-up little monkeys."

The first girl and I lay down in the other bed and tried to go to sleep. A little while later, I opened my eyes and saw the roommate standing in front of the mirror, putting on makeup and getting ready for work. She was wearing a tight, knee-length navy skirt, black heels, a sky blue uniform shirt, dark nylon stockings, and a little hat, which she wore tipped at an angle. The roommate was a flight attendant.

The other girl was awake, too, and we both watched the roommate as she put on her makeup.

"All right," she said before leaving. "I'm off to Rome. I'll see you tonight."

The ecstasy was starting to wear off and being in the room was making us hot and jittery. We got up, showered, put on our sunglasses, and went back to the party. Teddy was there, sucking on a Bacardi Breezer. The girl left us alone and headed to the beach where she danced absent-mindedly. I told Teddy about what had just happened to me. He was impressed.

"And how about you, did you do anything?"

Teddy looked around until he spotted a woman, which he then pointed out to me. She looked like a porn actress in the cheaper and dirtier kind of porn. She had a very dark tan and tribal tattoos on her lower back, and wore beach slippers with see-though high heels.

"Where did you guys go?"

"To the second floor of some bar," Teddy explained.

"Man," I exclaimed. "And you fucked her on the second floor of some bar?"

"I would've," he said. "But I had no condoms on me, and she didn't want to do it without a condom."

I took another look at the woman.

"Man, you don't want to do it without a condom either," I said.

"So she just blew me," Teddy went on. "But she did that thing where she took it deep into her throat."

"Cool," I said, then something occurred to me. "Did you come?"

"No. Are you crazy? Did you come?"

"No," I admitted.

After a while, being at the party also made us hot and jittery. We left and went to sit in a café in the center of Varna, while the music continued booming in the distance like an air raid.

"I'm going to call Koki in a bit and ask him to come pick us up," Teddy said when we sat down. "If I wake him now, he'll probably come here but instead of picking us up, he'll run us over in his car."

I didn't feel like drinking anything. We ordered beers. My beer tasted insipid, but at least it was cold. I pressed the bottle against my forehead.

"Man, what have we done to ourselves?"

Teddy didn't reply. Teddy agreed. When I took another look at him, he was asleep in his chair. His head fell forward and his chin touched his chest. He looked like he was dead, but I knew he wasn't.

I watched the people walking down the street for a little while longer and managed to drink half of my beer. Then I closed my eyes too.

*

Marietta was sixteen.

I met her in a dilapidated house in the center of Varna, only the outer walls of which remained. These outer walls were painted yellow and looked relatively well preserved, so it was possible to walk by the house without even noticing it. But on the inside, the house had no rooms, only piles of bricks and black circles that marked out old fires. At night, homeless people slept in it, and kids gathered there to smoke pot during the day.

I moved in with Marietta on the same day I met her. She was living with her mother, who at first wasn't thrilled with the idea, but then came around, presumably thinking that temporary cohabitation with an older young man might positively benefit the development of her daughter's character. It wasn't like I took up that much space anyway—all my belongings could fit into a beat-up yellow backpack, which I was in the habit of falling asleep next to, whenever and wherever the stimulants I was on started to wear off—on benches in waiting rooms, on the beach, on buses and trains.

Marietta and I lived together for a few days, during which we smoked pot almost constantly. Then we decided to go to the birthday party of a girl we knew from an online chat room. Her name was Smurfette and she lived in Nova Zagora. We decided to hitchhike. The first vehicle that picked us up was a horse-drawn cart, driven by two very black gypsies. The cart slowly drove along the side of the road, while the poor horse's hooves tapped on the hot asphalt mournfully. The gypsies stared straight ahead and said nothing. As we rode behind them, neither I or Marietta, who had very pale skin and hair that she'd bleached almost to the point of whiteness, said anything either. We were wearing sunglasses, and the gypsies weren't. After a while, one of them turned around and handed me a small plastic bottle, which still had a few centimeters of yellow *rakia* left at the bottom. I said thank you, took a long swig, and passed the bottle to Marietta. She also took a decent swig and gave the bottle back to the guy in front. We kept passing it around until all the *rakia* was gone, and then the cart's driver tossed the empty bottle into the shrubs and lashed at the poor horse with the leather whip to make it run faster. But the horse didn't want to.

Once we reached Nova Zagora, the birthday party wasn't hard to find. Smurfette's father was very wealthy, so he had bought up all the buildings and all the machines and equipment that had once belonged to the former communist agricultural co-op, and had then set up some sort of private farm. At one end of the paved square, between the agricultural buildings and the rows of parked combine harvesters, he had built a house for his family. The two-story house had big French windows, which at that moment were rattling from the music.

Smurfette was turning fifteen, or something like that, and her birthday party couldn't make up its mind between wanting to be either a teenager's birthday bash or a sinister techno party with combine harvesters. In the brightly lit kitchen of the new house, big plates full of finger sandwiches were quaintly laid out, reminiscent of the birthday parties from my childhood, while the cherry picker in the yard had been transformed into an improvised DJ stage. Two of Barabas's guys were spinning, and I knew them both. I climbed the cherry picker to say hello. One of them gave me a hug, while the other kept spinning, the tip of his tongue held tightly between his teeth in an effort to concentrate.

"Hey!" the first guy said. "How've you been, man?"

"Great," I said. "Listen, do you have any treats?"

"I have one candy left," the guy replied. "You want half of it?"

"I'd like the whole one."

The boy gave me a look of pretend reproach. I smiled. He smiled back.

"All right then, man," he said.

"What kind is it?"

He told me.

"That's great," I approved.

The guy carefully took the pill out of a little crumpled plastic pouch and placed it in the palm of my hand. He then licked the inside of the pouch and threw it away. I swallowed the pill with a sip of warm vodka mixed with black currant juice I was carrying in a plastic cup. I felt nauseous but gulped a few times and it got better.

"All right, I'll be seeing you," I said to the guy with the candy, then reached over and patted the other guy on the shoulder. "Good luck!"

"Why don't you spin a little yourself? You totally can if you want to."

I felt nauseous again. I gulped, looked at my cup, and threw it away.

"No, man," I said. "This is your guys' party."

I spent the next hour roaming back and forth between the yard and the inside of the house, drinking various drinks and exchanging brief words, hugs, or looks with people I either knew or didn't. I caught a glimpse of Marietta's face a few times, sharply outlined against the darkness by the strobe light, but only smiled at her and kept roaming around. A while later, Smurfette and I held hands and headed toward the gigantic, dark, incomprehensible buildings at the far end of the yard. We went inside some kind of a silo and sat down in the grain. We started kissing. Soon, I was trying to get Smurfette to lie on her back, so that I could get on top of her, but I got so nauseous that I quickly sat back up, put my head between my knees, and started gulping unevenly. Smurfette didn't say anything. She quietly caressed the back of my neck, then got up and returned to her birthday party. I stayed behind in the silo. The unfamiliar smell of grain was dry and comforting. I knew that if I managed to not puke for another few minutes, the bright and clear pulsations of the ecstasy would make their way through the violet alcohol shroud of the vodka mixed with chemical juice, and everything would be all right, at least for a few hours.

When I started feeling better, I hesitantly stood up and went out. The cold sweat quickly evaporated from my forehead, which caused me to feel an indescribable sense of bliss. The air outside was filled with different smells, but since the ecstasy had triumphed, they now seemed interesting rather than revolting to me. One particularly sharp and uncompromising scent was so unfamiliar that I decided to see where it was coming from. I walked alongside the silo's metal wall in the darkness, then past some combine harvesters and tractors, which stood there in the pitch black night like giant patient robots, and finally got to the source of the smell: a spacious cage made of V-shaped steel beams and chicken wire. Something large and whitish was living inside of it. When it heard me approaching, it lifted its head toward me and made such a low, throaty, and powerful sound that I inadvertently smiled. This sound had nothing to do with the cutesy "oink, oink" from children's books.

And so, this was how, in the summer of 1999, at the open-air birthday party of a techno princess from Nova Zagora, I saw a real-life pig in person for the first time.

Two weeks before the start of my mandatory military service, Bozhana called me on the phone.

"Hey!" I said. "How are you, Princess?"

"Great!" she said. "Ekaterina and I found an apartment, we're going to be flat mates. You should come over."

"When?"

"Tonight, if you want to."

"Should I bring anything?"

"Bring a gift," Bozhana said, and hung up.

I called Charlie and asked him to put me in touch with a friend of his who worked as a supplier to all the sex shops in the city. He gave me a discount on a double vibrator—a pink plastic ball with two average-sized penises sticking out of both sides. I also bought batteries. Then I had the vibrator wrapped as a gift, went home, did a few lines of amphetamines, watched a little porn on my computer, and in the evening went over to Bozhana and Ekaterina's house.

Everything would be decided in the first few seconds.

Bozhana and Ekaterina opened the door and I kissed them both on the cheek. The new apartment was beautiful. The two of them were very beautiful. I hadn't seen Bozhana for a while, and knew that Ekaterina had recently broken up with my friend Teddy. We sat down on the couch in the living room and I gave them the gift. My pulse was racing and my hands were slightly shaking, though I don't think it showed.

Bozhana and Ekaterina ripped open the wrapping paper and took the double vibrator out.

"Ta-da!" I said. "Your housewarming gift."

Bozhana and Ekaterina examined the vibrator.

"It's great!" Ekaterina finally said. "You want some white wine?"

"More than anything in the world," I replied.

"It's great, Bobby!" Bozhana also said, and kissed me on the lips. Then she turned to Ekaterina, "We'll have to come up with a name for it."

"Totally," Ekaterina agreed.

The two of them sat there, each holding one plastic penis between her cute little fingers. Bozhana was wearing clear nail polish, while Ekaterina's was bright red. Bozhana was sitting to my left and Ekaterina was to my right. I put my left arm around Bozhana's shoulders and started French kissing her. I felt Ekaterina unbuttoning my jeans, but didn't dare to look, for fear of jinxing the magic. I opened them only after I felt her hot little mouth.

The three of us were amazing, and afterward I left them to play with their gift while I went to a party where some friends of mine were DJing. Bozhana and Ekaterina's new place was so close to mine that I went by my apartment and did a few more lines of amphetamines on the way to the party. I couldn't believe the kind of stuff that was happening to me. I wanted to tell somebody about it, but couldn't exactly call Teddy, and it was already so late that Charlie was probably asleep, so he didn't pick up. In the club, I took an ecstasy pill but it seemed to have no effect on me. I waited a while, just to make sure, then took another one.

The second one didn't work either. I started to feel like my friends were playing really crappy music, while I'd just taken part in a mind-blowing threesome earlier that night, so I decided to go home, watch some more porn, and try to come using my hand.

On my way home, I suddenly started to feel the effect of everything I'd taken, all at once.

At first, my palms started sweating so quickly and so profusely that it was like I'd dipped my hands in warm water. Then the early morning's gray light suddenly burst into some kind of muddy radiance the likes of which I'd never seen before. The outlines of the objects around me became so soft that I was positive that if I happened to bump into anything, I would simply go through it. I spent quite a while breathing with my mouth open, simply because I didn't feel like lifting my bottom jaw to close it. Suddenly and without warning, bristling waves rose up from my legs, passed through my entire body with a ring, and opened up my skull toward the sky. When the second wave rose up, I bent over and tried to throw up, but nothing came out of my mouth. The convulsions were so strong that I thought I was going to shit myself. When I was able to straighten up, I felt so dizzy that I zigzagged down the street and had to lean on trees and cars along the way.

It occurred to me that I might die. I tried to take some precautions in order to prevent this, although at that moment the idea of death worried me not so much physically as theoretically. While stumbling back home, I took off my t-shirt and jacket and threw them on the street, and nothing in the world could make me bend over and pick them up. The thought of touching the warm fabric and holding it between my fingers until I got home made me nauseous again.

I was able to climb the stairs to my apartment, but by the time I got to the top floor I felt so light-headed that I also took off my pants and stood in front of the front door for a while, unsure about what to do. I could take off my boxers, too, and take a dump right then and there on the landing. On the other hand, I didn't want the paramedics to find a piece of shit in front of my door when they came. I stood there with my boxers down for some time, until the urge passed. After I struggled with my key for a while, I finally managed to unlock the door, so I went in, took the rest of my clothes off, turned on the shower, set the water to a cool temperature, and sat on the edge of the toilet seat with water pouring over me.

I sat there for a long time. By virtue of some chemical absurdity, I got sleepy. First my head started to droop, then I momentarily dozed off and slid down to the floor. I woke up when my knees hit the bathroom tiles, then got up and made my way to my room while I leaned against the walls. The room felt cool and airy. I put my towel over the bed and lay down, still wet. The water started to evaporate from my body. I swallowed, which felt like something I hadn't done in a long time. My hair was buzzing. My dick was shriveled like a tiny little pepper, but when I touched it, it sent a thunderbolt running through my body. I no longer felt like taking a shit or puking.

I picked up my phone and looked at it.

If I didn't call an ambulance, I could die.

If I didn't call a girl, I could be missing out on the best sex I'd ever have.

Bozhana picked up on the third ring. Her voice was quiet, still soft with sleep.

"Bobby?"

"Baby?" I whispered. "I need to ask you something. Come to me. I feel really sick."

Bozhana was a party girl. I didn't need to explain. She was quiet for a while, then said:

"You need me to bring you anything?"

I looked around without lifting my head off the bed. The curtains were drawn, there was a bottle of mineral water next to the bed, and a wooden box with condoms in it. Moving my eyes around made my whole face bristle with pleasure.

"No," I whispered. "Just yourself."

A week later, Bozhana and I decided to get tested for AIDS and STDs, so we could make love without having to use protection. I'd only done that once before, with Dena. At the clinic, they took our blood samples, then gave me a small plastic container I was supposed to fill with sperm. We went to Bozhana and Ekaterina's new apartment. Ekaterina was not there. We went into the bathroom and I unbuttoned my pants. Bozhana began caressing me and whispered something to me until I got turned on. Then she crouched, so she could get a better hold on it. She was quite good at it. I caressed her hair and quietly growled with pleasure. When I sensed I was about to come, I took it out of her hand and pointed it at the little container. Some of the sperm ended up where it was supposed to. Bohzana stood up and I embraced her as tightly as I could. My knees were trembling a little. It was very quiet in the bathroom, and our panting seemed to fill up the tight space. A few tears rolled down my cheeks.

"What's wrong, Bobby?" she whispered.

"Nothing," I said. "Everything's all right. I love you."

"I love you, too, Bobby," she said.

In the late afternoon, we sat down for a drink in a bar next to the clinic, to wait for our results. We had large dark beers, which quickly made us drunk. We looked at each other in the eyes and drank. We held hands and every once in a while I leaned over and kissed her.

"What are we going to do if we have AIDS?" she asked.

I finished my beer and held up two fingers to the bartender.

"If we're both sick, I don't think we should get treated," I replied. "We can take out bank loans or even straight up rob a bank, then run off to some island and live on the beach until we die. We'll drink cocktails and sleep in a hut. And we're not going to worry about anything."

"We'll live as if we're not going to die?"

"Exactly."

They brought our second round of beers, and I took a long sip from mine. Whenever I get drunk with a pretty girl in the afternoon, nothing seems impossible. I said nothing for a while, in order to make sure I really meant what I said. I did mean it. I really did want to run away. I really did want to not have to worry about anything. I really did want to live as if I wasn't going to die.

"Bobby?"

"Yeah?"

"What if it turns out that I'm the only one who's sick? Or that only you are?"

I gazed at the wall behind the bar. The small windows across from it were at the same height as the sidewalk outside, so the afternoon sun's slanting rays entered directly through them and cast blinding reflections on the polished wooden paneling. The bright light and the beer made the wood look like living gold. Did I really mean it? I did.

"We'd do the same thing," I said. "We'd still go to the island and have sex without protection, and then we'd carry on as planned, have cocktails on the beach and all that. At least we'll get to live a little. You want another beer?"

"In a while."

We sat there a little while longer, until it was time to get our test results.

On my way home, I walked by three girls with short skirts and shorts, suntanned legs, and tight tank tops, which revealed the outlines of their nipples. One of them was dressed in pink, the other in sky blue, and the third in yellow. The three of them were talking about boys and the seaside, but as I walked past, they fell silent and fixed their eyes on me. When they were already a few meters away, the girls burst into giggles. My ears turned red. I'd started crying as soon as Bozhana and I had said bye in front of the clinic, and by the time I was headed home, I'd completely lost it—my face was wet with tears and my mouth was trembling uncontrollably.

I went to the supermarket, bought a bottle of vodka and a bag of ice, and went home. I put on some music and continued drinking. Then I stopped the music and called Charlie. I was still crying.

"Hey, Charlie?" I said into the receiver and tried to laugh, but what came out was more of a sob. "I'm really fucked up, man. Can I talk to you about it?"

"I insist you talk to me about it," he said.

"Today, the wonderful Bozhana and I went to get tested for AIDS and all kinds of other stuff," I announced. "Actually, if we're being totally honest, they can't be sure about the AIDS yet, because it doesn't show up in the results if you got infected in the last three months, but they can tell you about all the other STDs straightaway."

I got up and poured myself some more vodka. I spilled some on the door of the fridge, then put some ice into what was left in the glass.

"And there's nothing wrong with me," I went on. "We're both totally healthy, man. We could get married and have kids, or whatever."

"Do you love her?" Charlie asked.

Tears started streaming down my face again. This time I managed to actually laugh.

"Thanks for the question, man," I said. "No. That's the really terrible part. I love Dena. I'll always love Dena. I want her back. I want nothing else. Do you get it? Nothing else matters."

Charlie was silent for a while. I started telling him about everything I'd had to drink since the early afternoon, but he interrupted me.

"Love is the answer to all questions, man."

"Easy for you to say. You believe in the soul."

"And you, man—don't you believe in the soul?" Charlie asked.

"I believe in the body," I said.

Charlie sighed, then said:

"I suggest you think about this question very carefully. What are you going to do now?"

I had a sip of vodka. The ice still hadn't cooled it down and the warm liquid flowed down my throat. It made me a little nauseous, but I was still able to swallow it.

"What am I supposed to do? My military service starts next week anyway."

"Yes, and you won't have to do too much thinking while you're there," Charlie agreed. "I meant tonight, though. Do you want to bring that bottle of vodka over, so I can drink some of it? I have the feeling you might need help with it."

"I don't know," I said and walked over to the window.

The room was dark but the moon was visible over the rooftops. Unsteadily, I turned around to look at the blinking digits of the VCR clock.

22:19.

"I was thinking of going to Indigo tonight, as kind of a farewell," I said.

"Man, I don't know if you should be going to Indigo, considering the state you're in," Charlie objected.

"Maybe I won't go then," I went on. "Maybe I'll finish the vodka and go to bed. Maybe I'll even go to bed without finishing the vodka."

"Call me if anything comes up," Charlie said.

"I'll call you if anything comes up," I promised and hung up the phone.

I sat there and looked at the moon.

22:21.

Somewhere far away from me, she was looking at the same moon.

22:22.

*